Heat curled where it had no place doing so as she remembered wicked eyes, and a man who had filled her early years with the hottest of fantasies—made all the safer for knowing Ram would never look at her that way. But she had to put all that to one side now.

Raking her dark cropped hair, Mia fixed her gaze on the bold print headline that had fired this crazy idea in the first place. *The Maharaja's Back in Town!* screamed the headline. Ram— or the Maharaja, as Ram was more popularly known—thanks to his heritage, his unbelievable good-looks and his money—not to mention his raw and dangerous sex appeal—was still her brother's closest friend, and he had been Mia's…

Childhood crush?

Susan Stephens was a professional singer before meeting her husband on the tiny Mediterranean island of Malta. In true Mills & Boon® Modern™ Romance style they met on Monday, became engaged on Friday, and were married three months after that. Almost thirty years and three children later, they are still in love. (Susan does not advise her children to return home one day with a similar story, as she may not take the news with the same fortitude as her own mother!)

Susan had written several non-fiction books when fate took a hand. At a charity costume ball there was an after-dinner auction. One of the lots, 'Spend a Day with an Author', had been donated by Mills & Boon author Penny Jordan. Susan's husband bought this lot, and Penny was to become not just a great friend but a wonderful mentor, who encouraged Susan to write romance.

Susan loves her family, her pets, her friends and her writing. She enjoys entertaining, travel, and going to the theatre. She reads, cooks, and plays the piano to relax, and can occasionally be found throwing herself off mountains on a pair of skis or galloping through the countryside. Visit Susan's website: www.susanstephens.net—she loves to hear from her readers all around the world!

Recent books by the same author:

Mills & Boon® Modern Heat™

RULING SHEIKH, UNRULY MISTRESS
SHEIKH BOSS, HOT DESERT NIGHTS

Mills & Boon® Modern™ Romance

MASTER OF THE DESERT

MAHARAJA'S MISTRESS

BY
SUSAN STEPHENS

First published in Great Britain 2010
Harlequin Mills & Boon Limited,
Eton House, 18-24 Paradise Road, Richmond, Surrey TW9 1SR

© Susan Stephens 2010

ISBN: 978 0 263 87750 2

Harlequin Mills & Boon policy is to use papers that are natural, renewable and recyclable products and made from wood grown in sustainable forests. The logging and manufacturing process conform to the legal environmental regulations of the country of origin.

Printed and bound in Spain
by Litografia Rosés, S.A., Barcelona

MAHARAJA'S
MISTRESS

CHAPTER ONE

SHE had to steel herself to place the call. Hard to believe she had once taken Ram on as easily as any tomboy took on her older brother's best friend, but a lot of water had passed under the bridge since then and these days Ram was a royal playboy.

While Mia had issues...

Scars and issues, as well as a desire to race cars again that refused to be repressed.

Get real, Mia. At least, don't lie to yourself. This is a chance in a million to see Ram again.

She hadn't spoken to Ram for...too long, anyway, Mia reflected as she waited for the call to connect. From what she'd read about him in the press she expected Ram to be as changed as she was. Ram had announced he would shortly be quitting his playboy life to serve his people in the independent state of Ramprakesh, but before that he was to enjoy one last indulgence—a timed rally car race across Europe in his super-car.

As soon as the newsflash came on, saying Ram's co-driver had been taken ill, Mia knew it was her chance to step in. Ram had to find someone in order to complete the last leg of the rally, which would take place in the winding streets of Monte Carlo—the same glittering locale where Mia had made a new life after an accident in a rally car had nearly blinded her.

She had believed she would never race again, and this was

a chance in a million to compete at the highest level, but first there was a little hurdle to overcome: she had to convince Ram to take her on. To do that she would have to be as determined and as pushy as she had been as a child. There could be no allowances made for the years that had passed—when and if he answered the phone she would have to launch straight in as if she were that same tomboy who had never flinched from baiting him...

Heat curled inside her as she remembered wicked eyes, and a man who had filled her early years with the hottest of fantasies—made all the safer for knowing Ram would never look at her that way. But she had to put all that to one side now. Raking her dark, cropped hair, Mia fixed her gaze on the bold print headline that had fired this crazy idea in the first place. The Maharaja's Back in Town! screamed the headline. Ram, or the Maharaja, as Ram was more popularly known thanks to his heritage, his unbelievable good looks and his money—not to mention his raw and dangerous sex appeal—was still her brother's closest friend, and had been Mia's...

Childhood crush?

Trying to force the lid down on that box proved impossible. Ram meant so much more to her than that—and was still as far out of her league as he always had been. The English edition of the *Monte Carlo Times* pulled no punches where celebrity was concerned and Ram Varindha needed no intro-duction, either to this playground for the rich and famous, or to the world. When a man was too good-looking or too rich, or he originated from an exotic land with which he shared an equally exotic reputation—and Ram filled all these criteria admirably—the glamorous principality of Monte Carlo was only too eager to welcome him home.

Mia's heart cannoned into her throat as a familiar black velvet voice growled a suspicious greeting.

'Ram?' She played it cool—authoritative and cool. 'Ram, it's me...'

Silence.

'Ram, it's Mia…'

'Mia?'

More silence as Ram no doubt trawled the telephone directory in his mind, running down the list of Mias until he came to one who lived in Monte Carlo.

'Give me a clue.'

So there *were* a thousand Mias in his life.

'Don't pretend you don't know me.' Her voice might sound confident, but beads of sweat were breaking on her brow—this was so much harder than she had imagined.

But not insurmountable.

Her life consisted of kicking down doors…

And licking wounds…

But she wouldn't think about those now, Mia determined, unconsciously adjusting the position of her jewelled eyepatch.

As I slipped under the anaesthetic I dreamed I was trying to stick an ice pick into Ram's cold, unfeeling heart, but his heart was a stone that bounced away from me, and when I woke up I was blind— She'd been having that nightmare a lot since the accident, and this was her chance to break free from it—a chance to put an end to the sense of desolation that had overwhelmed her when Ram had walked out of her life.

That had been years ago and she should be over it now. This was the best chance she was ever going to get to prove she wasn't over-faced by Ram, by life, by anything—and she wasn't going to waste it. 'Surely you remember me beating the heck out of you on your best stallion when you were careless enough to choose my parents to stable your horses with?'

'Mia Spencer-Dayly?'

Result—but could he sound any less enthusiastic?

'That's the one,' Mia confirmed, keeping up the bright act.

In fairness, she had never been the girl to whom boys' eyes were drawn, so Ram would hardly be eager to see her again. When other girls were trading style tips she'd been happiest mucking out the stables or hot-wiring the tractor. No doubt when other boys had been reading the *Beano*, Ram had spent his formative years mugging up information in the pages of a heavily illustrated *Kama Sutra*, but whether this crazy scheme of hers was mad, sad or just plain crazy, she had no intention of putting the phone down now.

According to the article in that day's newspaper—the one beneath the stunning shot of a tall, dark and unreasonably handsome hunk of a man with thick black hair and sharp black stubble—Ram had no intention of giving up on the last leg of the Switch-Back rally.

'What do you want, Mia?'

'What do *I* want? It's you that's in trouble, Ram.' She wasn't exactly home free herself, Mia realised as her gazed fixed on the newspaper shot of Ram with his thumb casually hooked through the belt loop on his jeans, long, lean fingers pointing the way to his number one attraction.

'Roll back the reel, Mia. Who gave you my private number?'

'I got it from Tom, obviously—'

She held back on the *duh*. One step at a time. She didn't want Ram slamming the phone down. On the other hand, she had to initiate the type of abrasive banter that had characterised their earlier relationship if she stood any chance at all of getting the best out of this conversation.

'What do you want, Mia?'

Her mind blanked.

'Did Tom ask you to call me?'

'No…'

'What, then?'

The five *P*s sprang to mind: *Proper Preparation Prevents Poor Performance*. But she could never have prepared for this. Covering the mouthpiece with her hand, she waited for her heart to slow down. Tom and Ram were as close as brothers, but Ram owed her no loyalty—they hadn't been in touch for years. No wonder he was suspicious. 'Today's newspaper?'

she said, regrouping fast. 'The article on the front page says you need help—'

'My co-driver's sick—wait a minute,' he said suspiciously. 'You're not suggesting—'

'I could help you—'

'You?' Ram exclaimed as if the world and everyone in it had gone mad.

'Why not me? I've got the right background.' Having won the junior section of several international rallies before the accident put her out of the game should put her in with a chance.

Shouldn't it?

Ram wasn't exactly biting her hand off, but if she was serious about this she had to convince him.

'You can't be serious, Mia—'

'I'm perfectly serious—'

'Forget it, Mia. Is there anything else? I don't have all day to stand and yap—'

'And neither do I, Knucklehead—'

'*What* did you call me?'

Ice cubes filled the air. And were just as quickly melted by amusement. Ram didn't have to laugh or say anything for Mia to know that the balance had tipped, and that everything was going to be all right now. They had catapulted back to a different time when squaring up for a good-natured fight came as naturally to them as breathing. 'Of course, if you don't want my help—'

'*Your* help?'

'I don't just meet and greet in a beauty salon, you know—I am a medal-winning rally driver—'

'Of Dinky cars, perhaps.'

She hid a smile. This was not the moment to turn the air blue. She was almost home and dry—she could feel it. And while she might have reinvented herself as a respectable meet-and-greet girl in Monte Carlo's most fashionable beauty salon,

Ram was an international playboy, so she had to raise her game and play it smart.

Ram, a playboy...

He'd always been heading that way—dark, sexy, dangerous—

'Are you still there?' he demanded as heat curled inside her, and far more insistently this time.

'I'm here...'

How did he live? Who was Ram these days—was he royal or a rogue? Was he a professional rally driver, or a professional bad boy? Ram had dropped off the radar around the same time she had, so she had everything to find out about him.

Secrets. What would life be without them?

'Just tell me what you want, Mia.'

'What *I* want? It's *your* co-driver who's gone down with a stomach bug—or maybe you scared the crap out of him with your appalling driving. Either way, I'm calling to let you know I'm here for you, Ramekin,' she finished sweetly, using the childhood name that had never failed to infuriate Ram.

'Like *I* need *you*,' he scoffed.

'Like, who else is going to volunteer at such short notice?' Mia countered smartly. 'Who else would want to spend the day cooped up in the world's smallest space with the world's biggest head? Who else won the junior section of the Davington rally that you know? And who's here now—?'

'In Monte Carlo?'

'No, dummy—New Ashford, Massachusetts. Of, course, Monte Carlo. Do you seriously think I'd waste long-distance charges on you?' She was enjoying herself now. It was a long time since she had crossed swords with the invincible Ram, and that had been back in the day when she had worn pigtails and had wielded a lollipop like a deadly weapon.

'Okay, let's meet.'

Ram's unexpected concession snapped her back to attention. 'Where?'

'L'Hirondelle.'

As it didn't do to appear too keen, she groaned. 'The stuffiest hotel in the world? I thought you might have changed by now.'

'Changed how, exactly?' Irony coloured Ram's voice.

'Oh, you know—ditched the pompous balloon in favour of a regular hot-air type favoured by most men—'

'L'Hirondelle,' Ram repeated. 'Six o'clock. Think you can make it?'

So he remembered her time-keeping problems. 'Can't we meet at the club?'

'Which club, Mia?'

She hadn't missed the weariness in his voice. 'You don't know?' she said, faking incredulous. Not to know the hottest club in town was akin to pariah-dom in Monte Carlo. Not that she would have known which club was hot that season had it not been for the girls she shared an apartment with. They were the type of pretty girls who kept their collective ears to the ground and knew everything worth knowing. Mia was the type of plain girl who had learned to develop acute hearing over the years. Wild? Yes, she'd been wild when Ram had left England, but in a driving too fast, riding too hard kind of way—the clubbing scene had never held any interest for her. Party girl she was not, but hopefully she could wing it. 'The Columbus?' She named the most popular club in the principality with the type of pity in her voice those in the know reserved for those not in the know—people like her.

'You go there?'

Careless. As if Ram wouldn't know the hottest place in town. 'You've heard of it?'

'Enough to know it won't be open at six.'

Second careless mistake. Not even the bar would be open at that time, Mia realised, remembering too late what the girls had told her. Plus she had to face the embarrassing fact that Ram was only arranging to see her early on in the evening so he had the rest of the night left to do his thing. 'I don't finish work until six—can't we make it later?' Giving her time for a major fashion overhaul courtesy of the girls—plus she'd need a wax, pluck, polish, fake-bake— She'd settle for a miracle. She might not be Ram's idea of a good-looking woman, but there was such a thing as pride.

'Come over to the hotel straight from work, Mia,' Ram said, ignoring her suggestion. 'I'll still be working on the car, so I'll be ready for some fresh air by then.'

Nice to know she would be a welcome substitute for an oily rag.

But she could still rescue something from the situation. The smell of hairspray filled the air here at the salon—and what little air was left to breathe was filled with the overwhelming floral scent-bomb of her employer's signature perfume. In his own way, like Ram, Monsieur Michel was a stranger to restraint. *Parfait.* Ram would love it here. *Not.* Throwing Ram off balance might be the one chance she had to persuade him to take her on as his co-driver. 'As I'm the one doing you the favour I think you should come here...'

And now she could only wait.

It was such a long wait Mia began to wonder if Ram had gone to sleep. 'Six o'clock at La Maison Rouge?' she prompted.

'La Maison Rouge?' he drawled as if she'd pulled him from reading a book. 'Isn't that the glitzy hairdressing salon on the main drag?'

'There's no need to sound quite so surprised.'

'I'm just surprised you're working there. What happened to your career in interior design?'

'Things...' Mia grimaced as she glanced into the mirror. Who would want to employ an interior designer with cheeks the texture of a rotting beam? Okay, slight exaggeration, but with her scars she wasn't going to risk it, whereas Monsieur Michel had dragged her in from the street saying she had the most fascinating 'look' he had ever seen—and she'd been too stunned by Monsieur's lilac eyeshadow to argue.

'Are you any good at what you do?' Ram demanded, snapping Mia back to full attention.

'I welcome clients into the salon, Ram. I book appointments. I call the clients by name—and I smile. Not much room for error there.'

'As long as they don't let you loose with a pair of hairdressing scissors.'

He was remembering the time she had chopped off the tail of his prize horse when she'd been a twelve-year-old grooming enthusiast. 'See you here at six?' She held her breath.

'Maybe...'

Was that a smile in his voice? The line clicked and died before she could decide.

Well, she'd thrown her eyepatch into the ring, and now she just had to wait and see what fate had in store for her—though there was nothing to stop her helping fate along a little bit, Mia concluded as she placed a second call to girls with more fashion savvy than she would ever have.

CHAPTER TWO

LIFE never failed to surprise Ram. Mia Spencer-Dayly turning
up out of the blue took him right back to his days at boarding
school in England when he'd been vastly attracted to the cha-
otic lifestyle of the Spencer-Daylys. As he'd been brought up
by servants, a family home, however disorganised, had seemed
like heaven to him, and when Tom had invited him back in the
holidays Mia had always been the main attraction—constantly
playing tricks on him, when everyone back home treated him
like a god.

But there was a puzzle here. He and Tom had kept in touch,
but Tom never mentioned his sister and he had never asked. He
and Tom had always respected each other's confidences, and
though he had often wondered about Mia, he hadn't wanted
to pry into her life. Yet here she was in Monte Carlo, offering
to be his co-driver—

Could he accept Mia's offer?

And open Pandora's box?

Mia was his best friend's baby sister and therefore untouch-
able, but there had always been a spark between them. Back
in the day that had manifested itself as constant taunting,
teasing, bickering—but now...

Mia was all grown up. And he was experienced enough to
know that if that same fire existed between them—and this
telephone conversation seemed to suggest that it did—that
persistent little spark could flare into an inferno—

Since when did he draw back from playing with fire?
This time he should—
And maybe he didn't want to.

Sex... Was never far from his mind, and he couldn't pretend he hadn't imagined taming the wildcat when they'd been younger. Mia's unaffected charm—her spirit, her quirky, contrary, upbeat nature—had always been enough to goad him to the point of distraction, and when the explosion came he fully expected the result to be everything it promised to be—

Which was why he must never touch her...

But it didn't hurt to meet for a drink. Plus Mia had always been one of the sharpest tools in the box and he could use a keen pair of eyes reading the route for him tomorrow. He might consider using her. Why not? He didn't want to pull out of the race at this late stage so he couldn't afford to be proud. And having won the junior section of several world class rallies certainly put Mia Spencer-Dayly in with a shout.

Monte Carlo equalled more, Mia mused, taking a deep breath as she prepared to start work at the glamorous hairdressing salon—more money, more glamour, more security, more everything. Definitely more intrigue than anywhere else on earth.

Which she would be adding to tonight when she met Ram—

When she met Ram...the Maharaja...

The man everyone was talking about. It hardly seemed possible. And what would her old childhood friend make of her new persona? She'd always been a bit of an oddball when it came to fashion, but her most recent look was what you might call a bit of a change from lollipops and pigtails...

As she examined her reflection in the mirror Mia remembered the day she had breezed into Monsieur Michel's salon to ask for a job. The canny old survivor had quickly guessed she had no qualifications in the hairdressing industry. She was only lucky that her noble-sounding name had got her foot in

the door. It turned out that Monsieur's troubled early life had
left him with a weakness for the sort of eccentric folk who
bumbled along the best they could in genteel poverty as Mia's
parents always had. Mia would be his meet-and-greet girl,
Monsieur had declared, removing at a stroke any possibility
of an amateur snipping dead ends from his duchesses.

Monsieur had seen the lot over the years, and instead of
turning his face away from Mia's injuries, which she dread-
ed—or gushing over her, which was almost worse—the eccentric proprietor of Monte Carlo's most glamorous beauty
salon had promptly renamed her Arabella, the Terror of the
Seas, after the infamous pirate queen, Arabella Drummond,
insisting Mia ditch her health scheme patch and adopt the
jewelled creation he had specially created for her.

The novelty of wearing a costume, of which the eyepatch
was just a small part, had held immediate appeal. The dressing
up box had been Mia's favourite escape at home—but this was
fancy dress taken to new and exotic flights of fancy. She hadn't
known such fabulous outfits existed, or could be made—but
then she hadn't had much experience of theatrical costumiers
before. Her dark, spiky hair lent itself to dramatic make-up,
Monsieur Michel had insisted—sympathetically leaving out
the fact that it also helped to cover her scars. So now she wore
a big gold hoop in one ear, tiny leather hot pants and thigh-
high leather boots, while an important-looking pad and pen
hung in a pouch from the studded leather belt she wore slung
low on her hips—not that there was anything written on the
pad, but Monsieur Michel said she had to be ready for all
eventualities—and if she was at a loose end she could always
direct her talents towards the skilful use of a brush and pan.

Like all his staff, Mia adored her eccentric employer and
knew Monsieur Michel's only purpose was to make everyone
feel welcome under his roof. He gave her the sort of non-
judgemental friendship Mia badly needed. The accident that
had left her scarred and blind in one eye had led to six months
of hell in rehabilitation, and had rocked her self-belief to the

foundations. It had taken time to rebuild her life and she hadn't done so quietly. She could never do that. She always had to walk on red-hot coals just to know she was alive. A winter working as a ranger in the frozen north out of touch of everything happening in the world had been just the start of her recovery. After that, she had come here, to the most glamorous principality on earth, where the language was French and the currency was good looks or money—and as she had neither, she wasn't exactly off to a good start—but she had reasoned that if she could make it here she could make it anywhere, and Monsieur Michel had helped her to make that happen.

Mia would be the first to admit that her new look was 'in your face'. It flaunted the fact that she was injured. There was nothing remotely apologetic about it. So she had a duff eye. So what? This was who she chose to be now. She had never been pretty, but at least now she had something that set her apart. Arabella Drummond? *Dead-eyed Tic*, more like, Mia concluded wryly as a muscle jumped in her damaged cheek.

Picking up a copy of that day's newspaper, she glanced one last time at the front-page photograph of Ram. With perfect irony, he was one of the best-looking men in the world. But there was a definite improvement, she decided, studying the picture intently. Perhaps it was the air of danger surrounding him…Ram wasn't even in his prime yet but he was clearly having fun getting there. Any sensible woman would run a mile…

Which was why she would be meeting with him tonight…

'No more mirror-time. You look beautiful, chérie, and clients are waiting.'

Monsieur's arrival meant Ram had to go on the back burner for the time being—not his seat of choice, but she had to concentrate on her duties, which wasn't going to be easy with the Maharaja in town.

But when Monsieur Michel swung the door wide Mia knew that loyalty to her employer would soon sort that out.

In Monsieur Michel's view of the world lay the root of his success. Monsieur could always see beyond the flawed shell to the person underneath. Beauty was in the eye of the beholder, he never tired of telling his staff. And Monsieur Michel saw beauty in everyone—

'Chop chop!' he exclaimed, shooing Mia ahead of him.

Neither of them was under any illusion as to why Mia was so valuable to the salon. They both knew there wasn't a woman in the place who wouldn't feel more beautiful when they compared themselves to Monsieur Michel's flawed pirate queen.

The trouble with Ram's rally car was sorted out sooner than expected. He took a shower and changed, and then his thoughts turned to meeting Mia. Why not bring the appointment forward? There had been far too many simpering, low-fat milksops in his life recently. Wasn't it time to take a walk on the wild side and eat some clotted cream? Mia had never made life easy for him and he was bored with easy.

Mia and he hadn't parted on the best of terms. The last time he'd seen Mia had been at Tom's engagement party when he had already known that his fate was cast in stone. He was to return to Ramprakesh and take part in an arranged marriage. It was how things were done—

How things used to be done.

He'd bought Mia a dress in Paris—a goodbye gift totally over the top, he realised now. In hindsight, that gift seemed little more than a crass attempt to soften the words when he told Mia he was leaving to get married and take up his place in a world she could never be a part of. A crass attempt at telling Mia he loved her and would always love her, but he had to give her up without ever really knowing her.

While they'd packed the dress he'd had a vision of one last dream night together. He'd been young then. He was cynical now and couldn't believe he hadn't considered the possibility that their dream night would go wrong from start to finish.

But that was then and this was now. And he was eaten up by curiosity. There were so many blank spaces to fill in between that night and this.

Monte Carlo was so much more than a race track, Ram reflected as he walked the short distance to Mia's place of work. The principality of Monaco was a tiny pink jewel, rich in culture and tradition set to perfection on an aquamarine sea. It was also a place where Mia was beginning to feel at home, he gathered. Five star plus suited her? It had never used to. Mia had always been dismissive of pomp and ceremony and all in favour of keeping it real. So what was she doing on the French Riviera where dreams were made of money? Or tinsel.

What wasn't Mia telling him?

He'd soon find out.

Perching on the staffroom window sill eating a doughnut during her break, Mia had almost managed to convince herself that with this type of view she could forget Ram—

Well, that was a laugh. Staring at another flawless blue sky was bliss, but it was overshadowed by a pair of mocking eyes. Was she up to this? She stared unseeing out of the window. Maybe she'd go to the beach later to chill out in readiness for meeting Ram. Ram would never go to a public beach, though the beach was fabulous. You could dream there—you could be anyone you wanted to be. You didn't have to go onboard one of the zillionaires' yachts in order to feel special in Monte Carlo. In fact, there were far fewer complications if you decided not to go onboard—

'You have a visitor, Mia.'

Mia's heart stopped dead. Monsieur Michel had just entered the staffroom. *A* visitor? There could only be *one* visitor. Who else knew she was in Monte Carlo?

'If you want I can send him away?' Concern clouded Monsieur Michel's face as he came close enough to see the shock on Mia's face.

'No— No, that's fine,' she said, licking the sugar off her fingers and rallying fast. 'I'll see him.' Springing down from her perch, she rinsed her hands in the sink. She wasn't going to turn this premature visit into a drama. Better to face Ram now and get it over with. She wasn't a child to be overawed by him.

No, Mia mused, catching sight of herself in a full-length mirror as she left the room. She was hardly Miss Sugar 'n' Spice these days.

CHAPTER THREE

'I HAVE made my private sitting room available to you,' Mia's kindly old employer told her with obvious concern.

'Thank you, Monsieur.'

'And you only have to tug on the bell-pull if you need me.'

Monsieur's concern was genuine and it touched her. 'Thank you, Monsieur, but I'm happy to see him.' On this occasion, a small white lie surely wouldn't hurt.

Bold resolutions were one thing; acting them out was something else, Mia realised, glancing anxiously around as she crossed the salon full of mirrors. Everyone else was carrying on as normal, which seemed odd until she remembered that their world was still turning at the prescribed speed. But why should she worry about how she looked or what Ram thought of her? This was her life and Ram could accept it or not. But he was in for a shock—and not just because of the unconventional outfit. She'd always been alternative where fashion was concerned, but she hadn't always been scarred. But she had wanted this. No one had forced her to make contact with Ram. She had wanted the challenge and the chance to prove herself on her own terms.

And it couldn't be worse than Tom and Ram's Leavers' Ball. The event had been held in aid of charity and was the hottest ticket of the year. She'd been sixteen, so of course she didn't have a date—she never had a date. She usually managed to frighten boys away with whatever outlandish new look she happened to be sporting.

On this occasion Ram had teased her into making up a foursome with her brother Tom and his girlfriend, when Ram's date had gone down last minute with flu. He'd even told her she looked lovely when they both knew that was a lie—she had cut her black hair aggressively short that year and had dyed some of the spikes pillar-box red—but the chance for the ugly duckling to turn up with a hot, eighteen-year-old prince and shock all those pretty girls had proved irresistible. Not that she had improved any on the fashion stakes. She could never compete with the pretty girls and so she didn't try. Her dress was a hand-me-down some well-meaning aunt had passed on to her mother. 'It's vintage,' she remembered telling Ram defiantly, pretending the ankle-length, sludge-green chiffon with its smattering of sequins was what she wanted to wear. Tall, hard-muscled Ram, acting like the prince he was, had shrugged and offered her his arm. Looking back, Mia guessed it must have been a charity event for him in all senses of the word.

But she was a very different person now—she could cope with anything Ram threw at her.

Which was why her heart was going crazy?

Opening the door onto Monsieur Michel's private quarters, Mia shut the bustle of the salon out. She needed a moment to clear her head and leaned back on the door. She and Ram hadn't parted on the best of terms. The last time they met had been at Tom's engagement party when Ram's behaviour had confused her. She had been so desperate for him to see her as a woman and had really taken trouble to look nice for once. They were both adults, Ram had told her when she had tried to engage him in conversation, and his life was moving in a different direction. He might have acted coolly, but he'd bought her a goodbye present—and there was even a moment when she'd thought he was going to kiss her, but nothing came of it. Why did he have to humiliate her like that? The dress was a parting gift, she'd realised later—a rich boy's pay-off for a childhood friend he would no longer have any time for.

She wasn't pretty enough or interesting enough to hold Ram's attention—she could see that now, but back then she'd been young and so very vulnerable. Ram leaving had been like a licence to run wild. The endless and ultimately unsuccessful search to put something in his place transformed her from daring tomboy to adrenaline junkie—treading the thin line between thrill and disaster became her only purpose, until the accident and an enforced stay in a burns unit brought her into contact with people far worse off than she was, by which time she was sick of her empty life and Ram was long gone.

And now he was back.

Courage. That was what the doctors had told her she would need after the accident when she had to face the possibility of losing her sight.

Courage. Did she have it? Did she have enough?

With Ram Varindha just a few feet away, it was time to find out.

And still she hesitated outside the panelled door. She had only visited Monsieur Michel's private sanctum on one previous occasion and that was for her interview. She remembered the room beyond the door being cool and pleasantly shaded. It overlooked a pretty courtyard that had walls coated in lush green vines and vivid purple bougainvillea. The décor inside the room could best be described as shabby chic, but its overriding theme was cosy. A couple of sofas faced each other across a well-worn rug, while gilt-framed mirrors dulled by time hung on expensively papered walls and an ancient grand piano rested silent in the shade.

Well, she couldn't stand here all day. Tilting her chin at a defiant angle, she seized the handle and entered the room only to discover that with Ram in the room Monsieur's cosy sitting room was anything but cosy.

Closing the door behind her, she remained in the shadows with her back pressed against the wall. How she wished she could turn the clock back—wished she could be someone else altogether—someone perfect and appealing.

Ram had no such inhibitions and had taken up the position of power in the centre of the room. Her spirit soared and rushed to greet him, and immediately drew back, sensing his aloofness.

'Mia?'

There was shock in his voice.

'You approve of my outfit?' She knew it wasn't about that. She knew the question in Ram's voice related to her eyepatch. And the rest. She lifted her chin, dying a little inside when she saw the expression in his eyes.

Quicksilver fast, Ram switched to his customary urbane manner. 'You never fail to surprise me, Mia. How long have you been hoisting the Jolly Roger?'

As they locked gazes, she realised that with perfect irony Ram's eyes were obscenely beautiful. *Even more beautiful than she remembered, just as he was infinitely more compelling. How could she have forgotten how attractive he was— how brazenly masculine?*

'I'm surprised to find you working here, Mia.'

'Oh?' She planted a hand on one hip. She refused to apologise or explain to this stranger, with his beautiful, mocking, all-seeing eyes, why she had chosen Monsieur Michel's salon as her sanctuary.

'I thought you hated all things flash?'

'Flash? I prefer to think of this as theatre.' She raised a brow as her old adversary's gaze swept slowly over her and did some assessing of her own. In jeans and a form-fitting top, with his bronzed feet naked in simple sandals, the aura of erotic possibility Ram threw off was alarming. He was every bit as tall and powerful as she remembered, and every part of him was lithe, toned and ultra-fit, but there was something cold in his eyes, and that was new. It was as if Ram had left the fun years behind—much as she had herself. She felt instinctively that this was not the hard-living playboy the gossip-mongers thought they knew so well, but a man who had experienced most things. It seemed the fantasy sweetheart of her childhood had turned into a tough, uncompromising man—and one who didn't even pretend not to stare at her injuries.

'I had no idea, Mia—'

'How could you?' She braced herself to walk deeper into the room…closer to Ram. Let him stare. 'I asked my family not to broadcast the news. And before you ask, I can do anything anyone else can do and probably twice as fast—providing I don't blink at the wrong time.'

She would wait a long time for any sign of the old humour, Mia realised. Ram just continued to stare at her, his brow furrowed as if he were reading everything she didn't want him to know.

Seconds ticked by. Her breathing sounded loud in the silence. Suddenly she was eight years old again and mesmerised by Ram. Or, maybe thirteen and feeling gawky with braces on her teeth. Or worse—sixteen, when she had wanted nothing more than the touch of his hands—

Apart from the braces, she was all of those things, Mia concluded as Ram eased onto one hip. 'I like the outfit,' he said. And finally his lips tugged in a grin.

'Your approval means everything to me,' she countered dryly.

She had laughed with relief when Monsieur Michel had personally orchestrated her costume at one of the more outlandish costumiers in the principality, but now she felt awkward and exposed, exactly as she had at Tom's engagement party. Why did Ram have to make those remarks—look at her that way—when he clearly wasn't interested? Who was he to come here to her place of work and judge her? So her outfit was brazen. What was that to him?

'Whatever happened to my girl, Mia?'

'She grew up.'

* * *

He had expected to feel many things when he saw Mia again, but he had not expected this—or the fierce desire to protect her that came with the discovery that his perfect imp had been so cruelly injured. Mia had always been defiant—always vulnerable—but her fighting spirit had always carried her through. Not this time, he suspected. She didn't fool him—she never had been able to do that. She had come to Monte Carlo like a beaten dog to defiantly lick her wounds—choosing the most glamorous place on earth to punish herself and ride the guilt. He had lived wildly too, but he had got away with it.

Why hadn't Tom told him? Why hadn't he picked up on this?

There was only one possible explanation. Mia's injuries must have occurred around the time he had been absorbed in his own private tragedy. There was only one certainty here—he couldn't leave her. He would have to make plans. All this he decided in a heartbeat as he stared into Mia's ravaged face.

'So,' he prompted dryly, as if none of these thoughts had occurred to him. 'We'd better talk about the rally. Are you sure you're up for it?'

'I have a problem with one eye, Ram. I'm not blind.'

He wanted to cheer at this proof that the old Mia was still in there, but instead he stared at her steadily as he explained, 'The last leg of the race is to be a time trial around the winding streets of the principality—'

'Which is why I'm perfect for it,' she cut in. 'I've only cycled the route, but I've lived here for some time and I know every curve and bump like the back of my hand.'

'So you could do it blindfold?'

She was shocked for a moment, but then she realised they were back where they used to be in the old sparring corral. 'If you're prepared to risk it, I am...'

'Then we have a deal.' He turned to go.

'Are you offering me the job?'

The uncertainty—the hope—in Mia's voice stabbed him to the heart. 'You'd better come through,' he warned.

'I will.' She held his stare.

What had happened to them both? Mia's injuries were obvious, but they were both profoundly changed.

'Just one thing, Ram…'

'Yes.' He held her gaze, enjoying the connection between them.

'Why are you racing cars when you should be running a country?'

He might have expected a counter-attack. 'Ah…' He shifted position.

'I know, it's none of my business—'

'Damn right it's not. I've had my finger on the pulse. I just needed one last—'

'If you say hurrah, I'll slap you,' she warned him.

This time he couldn't stop his lips pressing down with amusement. 'Still the old Mia.'

'Still up for a fight?' she demanded. 'You got that right.' And then her cheeks blushed red as if she could read his mind. The type of fight he had in mind right now was very different from those they had indulged in when Mia was younger.

'We should make time for you to take a proper look at the route map before you commit yourself.'

'Not that I need to.'

But he wanted her to—and not just to ensure she knew the road.

'Where do you suggest we do that?' she said.

'I'll *send* for you—'

'You'll send for me?'

'My driver will come and pick you up.'

'Forget it, Ram.'

'Do you want the job or not?'

'I want to work alongside you as your co-driver—I have no interest in becoming part of your entourage.'

'Make up your mind, Mia.'

Did she want the job? Would her heart slow down long enough for her to answer? Did she want a chance to return to the old days—the old ways—the fun, the heat and stress, the pace, the danger? *And that was just the rallying.* Did she want to spend time with Ram? 'If you're prepared to take your chances with a one-eyed co-driver…?'

Ram shrugged, but his gaze remained steady on her face. 'At this short notice I'll take whatever I can get.'

CHAPTER FOUR

THE encounter with Mia had shaken Ram beyond belief.
He was outside in the fresh air now, pacing the balcony of
his penthouse suite, but he had spent the first hour back
at L'Hirondelle with the phone welded to his ear, issuing
instructions.

He had never appreciated money and influence more. His
yacht was expected in harbour within the hour, and all the
other arrangements were underway. He wouldn't abandon
anyone he suspected of needing his help and he wasn't about
to walk out on Mia. The last thing she wanted from him
was his pity and he didn't need complications in his life, but
Mia's injuries had been a massive wake-up call. He'd been
easing himself into taking up the reins of a country—the
easy way, from a distance. He'd even ordered the building of
an eco-palace, which he would pay for with his own money,
and where one, as yet unspecified, day he had intended to
live…

All that had been brought forward. Seeing Mia again had
forced him to confront life's bigger issues. There was no easy
way for her—no long-distance solution. Mia needed close-up
warmth and support, just as his people needed him in the
country, rather than some distant stranger who issued orders
for others to carry out. He would return home and take Mia
with him. When he was sure she was healed she could leave
and pick up her life—become the old Mia, rather than this

theatrical version. It was the only way he could live with the
guilt. He should have been there for Mia—for the family—
for his best friend, Tom. He'd already been on the phone to
Tom, berating him—though that was hardly fair when Mia
had sworn Tom to silence. But since when had he been cut
out of their lives?

Since he'd cut the ties?

He couldn't have cared less if Mia had been dressed as a
fairy queen, complete with wings and a wand. The salon she
worked in was high camp and each member of staff had adopted some gimmick to set them apart. He was only sorry she'd
thrown away a promising career in interior design, though
he had to admit her new disguise was hot. Mia in Tom's cast
off clothes, climbing trees—Mia in a quaint, old-fashioned
ball-gown—these were both images he could live with comfortably, but Mia with the cheeks of her well-formed buttocks
just visible beneath a pair of tight black leather shorts—

So much for his good deed for the day! How quickly his
thoughts could turn from selflessly helping Mia to selfishly
wanting her. He had to turn his mind back determinedly to the
accident. She'd handled the fall-out well. He owed her respect.
Both of them had always liked to live dangerously and had
always played to win. He'd got away with it. Mia hadn't. He
stood by his offer for her to be his co-driver—that was if she
turned up for the race tomorrow. And something told him she
wouldn't be able to resist.

He was easing his muscles outside the entrance to the motor
racing club when Mia stalked up to him the next day. Wearing
banged-up jeans and sneakers accessorised with a shedload
of attitude, she was brandishing the fireproof clothes he had
arranged for her to wear. He noticed how full her lips were—
how kissable—

How firmly pressed together.

He was ready for battle when she stopped in front of him—

just as well. 'You knew what to expect,' he pointed out. 'You're hardly a stranger to the sport.'

'You should have warned me these came with your logo plastered all over them. I could have hired something plain.'

'You don't like naked women?'

She gave him a withering stare. 'When it's taken straight from the *Kama Sutra*, I draw the line.'

'This used to be a man's team.'

'Well, pardon me for having breasts.'

'Are we done?'

'You tricked me, Ram.'

'*I* tricked you?' he demanded, dipping his head to stare at Mia intently. 'It was your idea to help me—and you never asked about the clothes. Just kill the complaints, Mia, and concentrate on doing the best damn map-reading of your life.'

She muttered something unprintable.

'Just don't let me down.'

'Don't you let me down,' she retorted. 'We're supposed to be a team, remember?'

'The winning team,' he called after her as she marched off to get changed.

The helmet she had to wear for the time trial was about as sexy as a bucket with a viewing panel. White with a red stripe and a black visor, it had Ram's retro logo on the side. Five minutes into his life and she'd have to change that—not that she'd ever get the chance, Mia reflected. The all-in-one suit featured pants with a handy opening panel—

Well, she was used to that from her rallying days. Everything was fireproof, apart from her knickers—the one item of clothing that should have been fire-proofed if she was expected to sit next to Ram for any length of time.

And she had to stop thinking like that. Where had it got her back in the day—other than frustrated? It was time to stop thinking about Ram's sexual potential and put him in the correct box, which was temporary teammate. He was nothing more to her than that—and she was certainly nothing more to him.

It should get easier, Mia reasoned as she checked everything was zipped up tight. She could feel herself slipping into race mode, and once she was in the zone nothing would distract her from the job in hand. She had been good at rallying and would be again. And the chance to race with Ram, who was a world-class competitor, could only be another building block in her climb-back to confidence.

And those bold resolutions lasted all of five seconds when she emerged from the changing room to find Ram surrounded by adoring women. No surprise there—though he did have the courtesy to tear his attention away long enough to acknowledge her existence. Wearing a black baseball cap pulled low over his thick, wavy black hair and laughing eyes, and kitted out in race gear, he did look amazing, she had to admit—taller, stronger and far sexier than any of the other men in the competition—but it was the knowing curve of his mouth and the wicked glint in his eyes that promised more danger than any decent girl should want to get close to.

Irritated by all the hangers-on, she strode towards him like some warrior queen intent on relieving a siege, but the females currently assaulting Ram's defences had their radar working too, and perfectly coiffed heads swivelled as she came close—which was where the fantasy scenario faltered. Ram's glamorous admirers dismissed her with barely a glance—though Ram grinned as she elbowed her way through the scrum.

'Are you ready, Ram? Or would you like me to leave you here—to sign a few autographs, perhaps?'

His darkly amused gaze held hers for a moment. 'You'll have to excuse me,' he told his adoring fans without once breaking eye contact with Mia. 'It seems my co-driver needs a little last-minute reassurance.'

'Ha!' Mia exclaimed, swinging away.

No wonder Ram had insisted she get a good night's sleep before the time trials. Pity he hadn't taken his own advice.

She had a good idea of where he'd been last night—clubbing and who knew what else—though, unusually, there had been no mention of him in the newspaper, which had to be a first since Ram had arrived in town. But what did the media know? What did anyone really know about Ram?

What did Mia know?

Nothing.

Except the sight of women slavering round him made her feel sick. Good for him. Lucky for her she wasn't interested.

She hurried away—not even knowing where she was going—only certain she had to get out of there—

And jumped with shock as Ram grabbed hold of her arm.

'Time for the technical inspection,' he said in an altogether far too reasonable voice as he steered her towards the bank of officials.

She shook him off, but went willingly all the same. She was prepared to comply with anything connected to the race, but as soon as the formalities were completed this misguided experiment of hers was over. She needed a boost to her confidence—not someone to sit on it.

The moment she squeezed her rump into the moulded seat formed around Ram's rangy Danish co-driver's backside, Mia knew she had made a mistake. Ram in race mode was a powerful, brooding presence. She had not factored into her thinking how it would feel to be confined in such a small space with such a tightly wound mountain of a man. Had she really thought she would be cool with this? She slanted a glance at him—way too hot was closer to the truth.

'Ready for some real driving?' Ram demanded, revving the engine until she was sure it would explode.

She glanced at the impossibly complex array of dials and switches on the custom-built super-car and felt instantly at home. The answer to Ram's question was a positive yes. However she felt about Ram, this was a fabulous opportunity

to face her demons by hitching a ride with a true master of
the sport.

Dust and exhaust sparks flew as Ram released the brake
and slammed his foot down on the accelerator. G-force hit her
in the back like a punch. She had always been a speed demon,
but Ram liked to break the rules of physics—and for a split
second she was in such a state of shock she forgot what she
was supposed to do.

'Instructions,' Ram barked at her through the intercom,
followed swiftly by quite a few words she couldn't make out.
Fortunately for her sensibilities, Mia gathered, judging by the
aggressive set of his jaw.

She concentrated fiercely from then on, her gaze flashing
between the road and the map as she rapped out directions
as buildings flashed by in a silver rush. She couldn't help remembering her own rallying career when her arms and elbows
would have been flying everywhere by now. By contrast Ram
sat quite still, calmly driving the car—and not just with his
hands, but with his feet too, kicking the brake and hitting the
throttle in a fluent rumba of synchronized activity.

At least it seemed she was doing okay now, Mia thought
with relief. Ram's comments were on the brusque side, rather
than the rude. He was tough, terse and in control and there
was no false veneer of charm. She liked that. She liked him.
Far too much…

Ram exuded confidence and his confidence infected Mia
until gradually she found herself relaxing into the rhythm of
the race. He was totally on top of things and that was cool.
He knew exactly what to do under pressure, which was sexy.
She watched his hands move this way and that, making all
the delicate little movements that made so much difference
to their performance. He was the master of the elegant touch,
she concluded, wondering how that would translate in the
bedroom.

And which of the annoying females had he bedded last
night?

Maybe all of them?

She was only too glad to leave these thoughts behind and warn him about a series of hairpin bends, but then she returned to console herself that the other women were too obvious, too compliant, while she, Mia the Magnificent, would be like a lioness taming her mate—should she ever get the chance, that was. 'One hundred yards ahead—sharp turn to the right,' she rapped out. She had to forget what was beneath Ram's fireproof suit and fire off directions well in advance of him needing them. That was not to say a little day-dreaming was forbidden—just so long as she kept her concentration on the race. She was good at this. She hadn't forgotten what to do—and not even Ram was going to find fault with her technique—

And what about Ram's technique?

There was race tension—and then there was sexual tension. Her thoughts were operating on two levels, Mia realised. There was the race, and then there was something else sizzling between them. Could Ram feel it too? It was hot and tight—tight enough to unravel in a rush and sweep them both headlong into a situation. It was almost a relief when race excitement took her over when they streaked like a rocket down a rare straight stretch of the track.

Ram's hands on the wheel, the firm set of his jaw, the steady beam of his eyes—

Race excitement quickly gave way to something else entirely, though she yelped in panic when he took the next hairpin at outrageous speed.

'All right?' he rapped, placing his hand on her knee when she gasped.

Ram's brief touch was far more of a shock to her than his driving. 'Okay,' she rapped, not trusting herself to say more.

She pulled herself together as he accelerated out of the turn. Hairpin bends could come and go, but where Ram was concerned arousal was for ever. He was so good at this—the best. He had everything it took to be a top-class driver—power, strength and certainty, and there was no doubt that his timing was flawless. Lucky for her she had every excuse during the race to gasp and moan freely, as she imagined Ram's technique being transferred to a very different set of skills. With the roar of the highly tuned engine blotting out all extraneous noise she could really let herself go. Ram was everything she had ever looked for in bed—

In a driver, Mia corrected herself as they screeched round the final corner and Ram powered up to the chequered flag.

She exclaimed with relief as they crossed the finish line and Ram brought the monster machine to a screeching halt. Lifting off her helmet, she threw herself back in her seat, laughing with relief and happiness. The whole experience had been incredible—and quite an education. And the race had been good too, Mia conceded dryly as Ram removed his helmet and ruffled his thick black hair.

'You're still alive, then?' he said, turning to look at her.

Alive? She felt properly alive for the first time since…for ever. 'Did you see our time? According to my calculations we just knocked a good three seconds off last year's record.'

'Not bad,' Ram agreed. 'And good to see you did your homework,' he added wryly.

Would he expect anything less of her? Slanting a glance at him, Mia guessed not.

But then he started laughing.

'What's so funny?' she demanded.

'I think you must have forgotten that I can hear every sound you make through the headphones—'

'Every—' Mia's cheeks fired up.

'Every sigh and gasp—every sexy little groan you make,' Ram confirmed, staring at her with unbearable male smugness.

'Well, I can see why that might amuse you,' Mia agreed. 'Though…sexy little groan? I don't recognise that. I can only conclude you're going deaf and need to turn your microphone up.'

'And I'm equally sure you need your heat control turned down.'

CHAPTER FIVE

THE podium was bathed in sunshine. The crowd had gathered. The jeroboam of champagne that had been waiting on ice all day was ready to be uncorked and the winners were lining up. But Mia and Ram were still standing in the crowd. 'Ram, you should be up there—what happened?'

'Penalty points.'

'For what?' Mia demanded with outrage.

'Taking you on at such short notice. It was a wonder they let me race at all. My powers of persuasion,' he said to Mia's unspoken question. 'But these are time trials, so I lost out in the final calculation.'

'That's so unfair.'

'That's just how it is.'

'Ram, I'm really sorry.'

'Don't be. I wouldn't have been able to enter the race at all if you hadn't stepped forward.'

'Someone else would have.'

Ram shrugged, and it thrilled her to see his dark eyes glowing with amusement as he stared down at her. 'But I wouldn't have had half so much fun.'

'Hmm. So you don't mind our not winning?'

'I'll settle for a hug.'

The breath shot out of her lungs as Ram dragged her close, but then right on cue his glossy cheerleaders found them. 'Shall I leave you to your fan club?'

Ram laughed. 'You dare.' He steered her away from the squawking women.

'Are you using me to put those women off?'

He groaned. 'Am I so obvious?'

'Yep.'

'Can you bear to leave the trophy behind?' he teased her as they walked past the podium.

'Silverware needs such a lot of cleaning—but I still think you should have received some sort of prize. Your time was way faster than the rest.'

'I did receive some sort of prize,' Ram informed her.

How had she allowed herself to be talked into this? Racing with Ram was one thing, but now she was going out to dinner with him? Just the usual celebration after the race, Ram had assured her—and it had seemed rude to say no. There was nothing special about it—all the teams would be out tonight and it would look odd if she and Ram weren't seen about town—

Oh, really?

Frustrated? Her libido was pinging off the walls, which, admittedly, should have been all the warning she needed to turn down Ram's invitation, but he was so decisive and she was so... Maybe there were stronger women than her around— sensible, level-headed women, who would...

Who would definitely trample each other in the rush for the chance of a date with Ram.

She loved her flatmates, Mia realised when they greeted her at the door with squeals of excitement. 'We saw you on TV— You were great! So cool— The car was hot! The Maharaja was hotter than hell—'

She laughed as they dragged her inside, all talking at once. Mia had never been a girly girl, but her new friends had adopted her and treated her as one of them. They despaired of her refusal to follow trends, but lapped up her energy, just as they had lapped up Mia's emergency call demanding they find her a hot dress fast.

'We're going to clean up your act and send you out looking like a princess,' a pretty, dark-haired eastern European called Xheni who had recently been scouted by one of the top model agencies assured her.

'Princess Patch?' Mia suggested.

'Start with a shower,' Xheni insisted, ignoring Mia's comment as she bundled her towards the bathroom. 'You smell of engine oil.'

'Don't stint on the compliments.' Mia was still laughing when the other girls overruled this and, catching hold of her, dragged her the other way into their tiny, cluttered sitting room.

'You have to talk before you shower,' they insisted. 'And make sure you leave nothing out.'

Xheni was happy to concede defeat. 'I suppose you can sit and chat for a while. If it gets too bad we can always light a scented candle.'

Shrieks of unladylike laughter greeted this comment as they all collapsed in a heap on the sofa with Mia in the middle of the group.

'All right. I give up,' Mia announced. 'What do you want to know?'

'You can't just ring us and say you need a hot dress in a hurry without expecting us to conduct our own investigations,' Xheni explained, holding Mia down when she made a sly bid to escape. 'So stop acting cool and pretending like there's nothing special happening tonight when we all know you're meeting the Maharaja—'

'Who told you I was meeting Ram?'

'Ah, Ram,' Xheni said triumphantly, seizing on Mia's use of the notorious royal's first name. 'Guilty as charged,' she exclaimed, exchanging glances with their friends. 'Monsieur Michel told us, of course. Who do you think? He's so excited for you.'

Mia huffed dismissively. 'Well, he needn't be.'

'Come on—give us the juice,' Xheni insisted, ignoring Mia's protests.

The juice... Mia spared a moment for a wistful smile. If she had to go back to the beginning there were things she would rather forget—like Ram saying he would never forget her, when he clearly had for all those years. And now it seemed she was determined to throw herself back in his path again—and not like a naive schoolgirl with a crush, but like a deerhound on the trail of some juicy prey. Seeing Ram again had fired all her latent lust and directed it towards him like a heat-seeking missile.

Not that Ram was interested. Asking her out for dinner was just him being nice—

Ram nice?

Okay. To be honest, that didn't sound much like Ram.

'Have you known him for long?" Xheni demanded, breaking into Mia's thoughts.

'Long enough,' Mia responded dryly. Before the accident she would have been thrilled at the thought of tonight, but the loss of her sight had changed all that, reducing her to a shambling, petrified wreck who was frightened of her own shadow—or who would have been, if she could have seen it—

'Coffee, anyone?' Xheni said as one of the girls carried a tray in. 'I don't know about you lot, but I'm settling in for a very long and tasty session...'

Mia stared at the steaming mugs, remembering that after the accident even silly little things like learning to carry a tray again had become a mountain she'd had to climb in terror. But like the girls Ram had taken her injuries in his stride. He didn't appear to find them repulsive. He didn't pity her either. In fact, he gave no quarter, which was why she was so comfortable with him—

Comfortable? Did that explain a rocketing heartbeat when she thought about him?

'Have you collected your thoughts?' Xheni prompted.

Her thoughts had been in disarray since the rally. She could never have predicted that one phone call to Ram could change her life, forcing her to ask herself all sorts of questions.

'Don't look so worried,' one of the girls said, putting her arm around her. 'We promise to fire questions at you only until we run out of them.'

Mia had to laugh. 'And that's likely to happen.'

She should stop worrying and take this as a sign of how far she'd come. The girls had been part of her recovery and she was grateful to them. She'd lost her confidence along with her sight and had asked everyone, including her family, to leave her alone while she worked out how to go forward. How could an interior designer face the world blind? How could *she* face the world blind? When the sight in one eye returned she should have been grateful. She should have been down on her knees thanking God for his mercy. She had her life, her health, and the sight in one eye. Wasn't that enough when she could so easily have been killed? But she hadn't felt grateful. She had felt bitter and depressed, and had only wanted to spare those who loved her from the fallout, and so she'd left home. Her dream of leaving her mark on the world had felt as if it was over. And as for her dream of sailing into the sunset with a man like Ram Varindha—

Well, he'd hardly want her now, Mia reflected, checking her eyepatch was in place.

'Well, come on, then,' Xheni prompted. 'Tell us about the Maharaja.'

How could she begin to tell them about Ram when he had flashed across her world like the brightest of comets leaving her to clutch in vain at his sparkling dust? When Ram had left England she'd known she would never get over it. There would be no more ridiculous birthday cards, or phone calls requesting a taxi for a maharajah and his elephant—no one twanging her old lute, or whistling 'My Girl' ever again—

'Start with how you came to be driving in the rally with him,' one of the girls insisted.

'Or how you came to know Ram would be driving in it,' Xheni interrupted, wide-eyed, nudging her friend. 'Well, we're waiting,' she said as one by one the girls settled down. 'We want to know everything about Ram. And you can leave out all the boring bits like what he likes to eat—unless that's you.'

The girls had completely thrown her out of the past and into the present, and as they laughed their agreement she spluttered, pulling a face. 'I'm hardly his type.' Putting it mildly.

'Who says?' Xheni demanded. 'Have you ever put him to the test?' Resting her chin on the heel of her hand, the pretty young model leaned forward.

'And how am I supposed to do that?'

'Hold his gaze... Moisten your lips...'

The girls cheered as Xheni gave a practical example.

'That would have worked well if I'd tried it out on a hairpin bend—' And was easy enough for Xheni to say. Like all the girls Mia shared an apartment with, Xheni was stunning and accepted male attention as her due. 'Anyway, I'm sure he's got better things to do—'

'Which is why he asked you out on a date,' Xheni interrupted.

'It's hardly a date,' Mia argued. 'It's more of a debriefing session.'

'Excellent!' Xheni screamed to filthy laughter from the other girls.

'Believe what you will—'

'Oh, we will,' the girls assured her, exchanging glances. When Ram was in town there was a buzz of sexual excitement in the air; they'd all felt it.

'I still want to know how you came to fall for Ram— because you have,' Xheni insisted, looking to the other girls for agreement.

'We all have,' they chorused, hugging themselves as their vivid imaginations got to work.

'What about the rally?' Xheni prompted. 'What did that feel like—pressed up close to him in such a highly charged and dangerous situation?'

Mia pretended bewilderment. 'We were professional,' she protested, blushing. 'How either of us felt about the other had nothing to do with the rally—we just got on with it—'

'Yeah, yeah,' the girls chorused.

Mia wasn't ready to admit how she'd felt—or that she was still coming to terms with how deeply Ram had affected her.

'A professional situation, huh?' Xheni teased her. 'Okay, so let's start at the beginning and work up to that boring old professional bit.'

Mia shrugged. What could she tell them?

All the bits she didn't allow herself to dwell on—like filling in the gaps of Tom's engagement party? *When selecting an appropriate look for the evening hadn't involved finding a suitable eyepatch to wear with her going-out dress...*

'Ram was my brother's school friend, and things really came to a head on the night of Tom's engagement party—'

'Sex was in the air,' Xheni advised the other girls.

Mia shook her head firmly. 'We're talking about my brother and his wife. Love was in the air—'

'Even better,' Xheni approved.

The other girls sighed theatrically, but their mischievous glances weren't lost on Mia, who sat up. 'If you won't be serious,' she warned, pretending stern, 'I won't tell you anything.' She waited for silence, realising just how long she had shut out the details of that night. 'I was all dressed up in my party frock—'

'White lace and silk ribbons,' one of the girls supplied dreamily.

'We were scholarship kids, remember? My parents lived on the breadline, and even if they did keep up appearances in the crumbling family pile the best they could do for me was a hand-me-down with a rip beneath one arm that my mother stitched up for me. The dress was faded blue and the only thread my mother had was red, but she assured me no one would notice.'

'Except Ram did,' Xheni guessed.

'Because he couldn't stop looking at you,' another girl suggested with a sigh.

'Only to check I wasn't chewing gum. Anyway, who's telling this story?' Mia demanded.

'Go on,' the girls begged her, thoroughly enthralled now.

'Okay,' Mia agreed, sighing as she remembered. 'When Ram arrived I was surprised when he took me to one side.'

'But you quickly adapted to this new development,' Xheni said hopefully.

'Of course. I explained I couldn't leave the entrance hall,' Mia continued, refusing to be sidetracked.

'What?' the girls demanded to Xheni's moan of despair.

'My job was to greet my parents' guests and show everyone where to go.'

There was a chorus of groans, which Xheni quickly shushed.

'Ram insisted on seeing me in private—and so I showed him into the library.'

'The library?' Xheni exclaimed with despair, but when something wistful came into Mia's face all the girls fell silent.

'Ram had changed somehow—and in a way that frightened me, because it changed everything between us. He was cold, and yet...not cold. At least, his eyes were hot.' She bit her lip as she remembered. 'He'd bought me a dress from Paris—a dream of a dress. I'd never seen anything like it before except in magazines. It was my first full-length ball gown. He'd guessed my size and everything,' she added with innocent surprise, but this provoked a chorus of laughter.

'I have to say Ram's good with figures,' Xheni exclaimed,

clutching her chest as she gasped for breath. Reaching for a
nearby newspaper, she brandished the front page that esti-
mated Ram's fortune in billions.

'Go on,' the other girls encouraged Mia.

'Ram told me to go and put the dress on so he could see
me wearing it.'

'And, of course, you obeyed him?' One of the girls suggested, with a wink.

'No,' Mia said quietly. 'Actually, I refused.'

'You refused?' Xheni demanded to a murmur of disapproval from the other girls.

'I didn't want to upset my mother—I didn't want her to
think that the dress she had so carefully mended wasn't good
enough for me.'

The girls looked at each other, understanding. None of
them had enjoyed easy lives.

'Do you still have the dress?' Xheni demanded.

'I think it's still at home somewhere. I didn't want to offend
Ram either, and so I thanked him for his lovely gift and put
it away upstairs.'

'And you've never worn it since?' Xheni guessed.

'No, I never have,' Mia confirmed, remembering back to
how she'd reverently untied the black silk bow on the powder-
pink gown box and lifted out the exquisite dress Ram had
bought for her from its nest of ivory tissue paper, knowing she
would never wear it. Holding it up in front of her body, she
had stood in front of the mirror pretending Ram was holding
her and they were dancing.

And the rest…

What she could never have imagined was that Ram would
come to find out what was keeping her. 'You haven't changed
your dress,' he had accused her when she answered his rap on
her bedroom door.

'There isn't time for me to change,' she had lied, trying to
force the door closed—which wasn't an easy thing to do when
there was a maharajah's foot in the way.

Ram's dark eyes had called her a liar and when she had given up on the door and tried to slip past him he'd caught hold of her and pinned her to the wall, demanding, 'You don't like it, do you?'

Ram had always teased her, but on this occasion his face had been very close—and she hadn't been a baby any longer— or a tomboy to be teased. And had he even been talking about the dress? She had been too naive to know. She could only remember that Ram's eyes had been full of teasing laughter and there had been a dangerous frisson of something running down her spine, and her head had been full of thoughts of her bed just a few tantalising feet away from them—

'You only have to say if you don't like the dress I bought you,' Ram had murmured, his lips so close to her own that hers had tingled.

'I love it.' And then she'd been angry when Ram had straightened up and pulled away—angry with herself for being such a girl when Ram was already a man. If she had been one of the older girls with her eye on him, she would have shut the door with both of them on the bedroom side of it.

'If you love it so much, why aren't you wearing it?' Ram had demanded while running the fingertips of one hand very lightly down her arm.

Even as her whole body had filled with heat Mia had kept her cool. 'I love the dress you bought for me, Ram, but I prefer the one I'm wearing.' And with one last defiant glance she had slipped out of his grasp.

But Ram had been too fast for her. Catching hold of her arm, he brought her in front of him. 'I wanted to be the one to choose your first grown-up dress.'

'Well, you did—and when you start treating me like a grown-up I'll be sure to wear it.'

Mia could still remember the buzz it had given her to flirt with Ram. She had never courted danger quite so avidly before. She had never realised how dangerous Ram could be. She had teased and provoked him on many occasions, but on that night she had been purposefully pushing it. She couldn't have known that this exhilarating encounter was heralding the end—or that Ram had only bought her the dress as a goodbye gift. He had gone on to explain as if she were still a child that he had wanted to buy her something special before he left to take up his place in the world. And when she had accused him of being pompous he had turned cold—colder than she'd ever known him as he told her that from that night everything must change—

'Why must it?' she had demanded like a spoiled child. When you were young, you couldn't imagine things changing and Ram had always been part of her life.

'Did he kiss you then to console you?' Xheni demanded, jolting Mia back to the present day.

'Ram was not my age—my class. We were impoverished. He was not. Ram came from a long line of noble maharajahs, whereas I came from a long line of scoundrels.'

'And all the more interesting for it,' Xheni insisted with a flick of her hand. 'I think you're making excuses,' she said, exchanging glances with the other girls. 'I think you like Ram a lot more than you're prepared to tell us.'

'He was a childhood crush and nothing more—he was my brother's friend—'

'That all sounds like excuses to me,' Xheni observed crisply.

'I'm not making excuses—I'm telling you how it is. I would never dream of impulsively kissing a man so much older than me—especially one who was destined to embark on such a very different path through life.'

All this was true. She had always been bold, but she had never been stupid. At least, not until the night Ram left, when she had turned on the self-destruct switch, wanting nothing more than to court danger until there was no pain left.

What a waste of an eye that had been. Ram had never left her mind once—or her heart—and the pain of losing him had only increased on the day of the accident when she'd lost her sight.

'Well, Cinderella,' Xheni insisted, dragging Mia back to the present day. 'Tonight you shall go to the ball…'

'Oh, no—I couldn't possibly borrow that,' Mia protested as Xheni brandished one of her most recent catwalk trophies. She knew the girls liked spoiling her, but she had never expected a gesture like this. 'It must be worth a fortune.'

'It is,' Xheni assured her, shaking out the flirty-length column of coral silk. 'And it will look perfect on you—don't argue. I'll soon have plenty more where this came from.'

'But you've only recently—'

'Changed careers?' Xheni glanced out of the open door across the hallway to where her waitress's smock hung freshly laundered on a padded hanger inside the doorway of her room, ready to return to the hotel that had employed her until she got her big break.

Mia glanced from the neatly pressed smock to the hot dress Xheni was holding out to her. The padded hanger alone, judging by its fancy logo, was probably worth far more than Xheni's redundant polyester uniform.

'Let's have some confidence, shall we? Both of us?' the young model prompted, standing up. 'Now, go have that shower…and come out smelling of—'

'Roses?' Mia suggested tongue in cheek.

'Anything but engine oil,' Xheni exclaimed, pulling a comic face.

CHAPTER SIX

MIA took her time in the shower, luxuriating in suds, refusing to let anything, least of all Ram Varindha, to interrupt her me-time—though she did caress her breasts and imagine it was Ram's hands stroking them. But apart from that...

'Mia,' Xheni called out helpfully from behind the bathroom door. 'Ram's here to see you—'

'What?' The steaming water continued to thunder down, while Mia froze mid-expletive with her elbows pointing sky-wards and her fingers planted securely in the bubbly tangle that was her hair. 'What do you mean, Ram's here? He's sup-posed to be sending his driver.' When there was no reply, she switched off the shower. She could only hope that by some miracle Xheni was mistaken.

'The Raja's here,' Xheni whispered through the door. 'I showed him onto the balcony so he wouldn't have to look at our mess.' Xheni laughed.

Mia didn't laugh.

There was a pause and then Xheni added in a louder voice, 'Mia, are you all right in there?'

''M okay,' Mia managed, fighting off a breakdown. Her frantic gaze tore around the tiny bathroom, locating towels, clothes, her toothbrush and some paste—

'Isn't it great Ram's come round to see you?' Xheni whis-pered happily. 'But don't be too long in there, Mia. It's threat-ening rain and he's standing outside.'

There was another pause—much longer this time.

'Are you sure you're all right in there?' Xheni demanded. 'Mia—please answer me—I'm starting to worry…'

'Just leave me to get dressed—I'll be as quick as I can— promise—' This promise was made as she cannoned off one wall and then the other in her desperate rush to get some clothes on.

'There's a lot of noise in there.' Xheni sounded concerned. 'What are you doing?'

Struggling to pull on her clothes without wasting time drying herself? Right now she was hopping frantically with one leg in her knickers while she cleaned her teeth at the same time.

'Mia, can you hear me?' Xheni demanded anxiously. 'That was thunder—and Ram's standing…on…the…balcony.'

'I can hear you, Xheni,' Mia shouted between spitting, swilling and wiping her mouth. 'Tell him I'll be right there.'

'The girls and I are on our way out,' Xheni called back. 'Why don't you join us? We'll be at the Dragon Club—chocolate martinis. How can you resist? Bring Ram along—'

'Xheni, wait—don't leave me alone—'

Too late. The front door had just closed on a world of giggling.

She was on her own.

With Ram.

She calmed herself. She would not rush. If Ram had changed the arrangements without consulting her, then Ram could damn well wait. Meanwhile, she had some serious thinking to do.

She took extra care with her appearance, loving the cool, slinky dress Xheni had lent her for the night. The coral silk felt sensational against her skin, and the figure-hugging couture cut ensured it flattered every part of her. She needed all the help she could get, Mia concluded, checking her eyepatch was still on the shelf where she'd left it. She teamed the dress with some pretty, strappy sandals and then thought about make-up.

She studied her naked face in the mirror. One eye was cloudy, the other clear—a bit like life, really, Mia concluded. One moment she knew exactly what she was doing and the next she was in a fog. The only certainty was, no way was she leaving this bathroom with her tail between her legs. But she would fix her eyepatch in place.

With these thoughts under her belt she started with lip gloss, applying it carefully before adding some smudgy grey shadow to the eye on show. She had left her hair in the soft curls it customarily fell in when she didn't spike it up with gel, and after a flirt with the mascara wand she was ready... pretty much. She checked her appearance one last time, craning her neck to see a rear view. Then drawing a deep breath, she buckled on her mental armour and went to find Ram.

When she entered the small sitting room Ram was standing on the balcony. He turned the moment he heard her come in. Slipping his sunglasses down his nose, he took one look at her and stowed them in his pocket. Smiling faintly, he murmured, 'Mia...'

'Will I do?'

He pretended to consider this—the rasp of thumb on stubble drawing her attention to his sexy mouth. 'Different? Quirky? Refreshing?' he said. 'Yes. You'll do.'

'You make me sound like the latest design-led power shower.'

'It could be worse,' Ram countered, his lips pressing down attractively as he shrugged and held her gaze. 'I could have likened you to a little ray of sunshine—and I just know how much you'd love that.'

'You wish,' she said, raising a brow. 'You clean up well too,' she observed casually.

Major understatement. Ram looked hot in nothing more exciting than plain dark trousers and a crisp checked shirt. It was how he wore them that made the difference—elegantly—casually—hot-chic couture on the hottest of fit bodies. You didn't need anything more than that. And then there was the heavy-duty belt that cinched his waist, drawing her fascinated gaze down over his rock-hard belly to his—

'Are you ready to go?'

'Of course,' she said, refocusing rapidly. 'I'll just stick my purse in my handbag.'

'You're paying? Even better,' Ram observed with amusement in his rich, husky baritone.

'Taxi fare home, actually—my mother told me I should always have it.'

'Your mother was right.'

'Won't be a moment,' she threw over her shoulder as she exited the room.

The truth was, she needed a moment to cool down and collect her thoughts. Leaning back against the door, she drew in a deep, steadying breath. This was madness—

This was inevitable. So why pretend it was anything else?

'Just coming,' she called, quelling her excitement at the thought of all that hard-muscled flesh awaiting further investigation. Not that she'd get a chance, but a girl could dream, couldn't she?

He stared at Mia when she came back into the room. Even with her hair cut short she looked lovely, and, with her gamine features and piquant style, very French. But where did she get that dress? Initially, he'd been impressed by the traffic-stopping outfit and it had pleased him to think Mia had chosen to go to such an effort for their night out. The beautifully cut dress screamed couture, but it was a gown that, however successful a meet-and-greet girl Mia might have become in such an improbably short space of time, she would never be able to afford...

Suspicion coiled deep inside him. Mia might have grown

up and she had certainly been bruised by life, but she had always had a wild streak. Had some man bought her favours with pretty clothes? Fury snapped inside him. And joining it was lust.

He put the anger aside, telling himself that who she spent her time with was none of his business. He had no interest in investigating all the ins and outs of Mia's life—none at all—

And if he believed that, Ram concluded as Mia's warm, soft body brushed his when they made a theatrical play of linking arms before they left the apartment, then it was time for him to touch base with reality.

The clouds had lifted by the time they stepped outside, and the evening promised to be warm and fine. 'Where are we going?' Mia asked Ram as he prompted her to turn down a cobbled alleyway in the direction of the waterfront.

'To celebrate.'

Vague or what? The girls had told her Ram's yacht was in the harbour—'Ram's floating city' was how they had described it, begging Mia to somehow blag a guided tour. She'd try, she had assured them, assuring herself even she wasn't that mad; going on board a billionaire's yacht was something she had promised herself she would never do—especially not Ram's.

But right now he was guiding her towards one particular and very famous doorway. 'The best club in town?' she said nervously.

'We talked about it.'

'And you know I hate clubs.'

'You'll be fine with me.'

Would she? As soon as she recognised their destination, Mia could think of a thousand reasons why she didn't want to go there. She wouldn't be able to relax in case she made a fool of herself. She might be dressed up to the nines thanks to the girls, but she was clumsy and totally lacked sophistication.

There would be the usual clutch of royalty and celebrities—and don't even get her started on her scars, when all the glamorous patrons would be paparazzi-picture-perfect. And she was with Ram, who was hardly inconspicuous… 'What have I done to deserve this?' she murmured anxiously as the doorman saluted Ram.

'Beats me,' Ram replied dryly as he ushered her inside.

The heat of the club rose up to envelop them and it was laced with an exotic mingling of scent. Ram held her arm all the way down the dimly lit steps and she was glad of it as she picked her way in Xheni's stratospherically high heels. The dark, womblike cave was packed, Mia realised with alarm, but everyone made way for Ram. And now music was throbbing through her—familiar music. 'Motown?' she demanded, turning an accusing stare on him. 'So you didn't set this up?'

'Me?' he said, pressing his hand to his chest as he gave her his best shot at an innocent look. 'Along with the crowd of extras?' he suggested as another well-known prince sauntered by.

'I don't believe you.'

'That's up to you.'

She felt a thrill of anticipation as Ram's hand tightened on her arm. 'I'm not going to lose you in the crowd,' he promised, steering her forward.

As if she were going to leave his side, Mia thought, wondering if every tiny hair on the back of her neck was going to remain permanently erect.

'Motown night is always the most popular,' Ram explained as the maître d' came hurrying forward.

'And you didn't have a thing to do with it,' Mia commented dryly. 'It was by sheer chance that the DJ happened to be playing my favourite music when I walked in.'

'It's a good job I'm back in your life,' Ram observed, shooting Mia a devastatingly stern look. 'You've become far too cynical since I've been away.'

'You mean, I'm not as gullible as I used to be,' she countered.

Ram was quite an operator—if you liked your men straight up. A non-alcoholic cocktail seemed a safer bet to Mia right now—though, admittedly, not half as interesting.

And guess what? The owner of the club had personally reserved the best table for them—a table that enjoyed an even more advantageous location than the table occupied by the other prince and his party, Mia noticed. 'So they spoil you here too?'

'Champagne?' Ram suggested, curbing a grin.

'Orange juice for me,' Mia said primly.

The DJ chose that moment to play a new track. *Heatwave?* No kidding.

A jug of orange juice later and Mia was finally starting to relax. Ram had been nothing but relaxed, and he was seemingly unaware that he had the undivided attention of every woman in the club—

Did she say relaxed? Ram had just leaned forward to ask her if she loved him! 'I beg your pardon?' she exclaimed, leaning back.

'"Do You Love Me"—great tune.' Ram's ridiculously handsome face creased in a grin.

She slid him a disapproving look. 'Very nice.'

'Do you wanna dance?'

'Song title or action?' she demanded. As Ram cupped his hands around his mouth to yell above the music she was determined not to be caught out a second time.

'Action,' he said, standing up.

Dance with Ram? Dance with the most dangerous man on the planet. There were surely more dangerous pursuits she had indulged in—but she couldn't think of one right now.

'Unless you're scared I'll show you up?' he suggested.

'As if.'

Ram was already on his feet and reaching for her.

So why was she still hanging back?

Maybe because the dance floor was heaving with the type of people who regularly graced the front page of the world's leading society magazines all currently performing their own heated up version of the twist—

So? She could do no worse than fall flat on her face.

It was only a short step from their table to the dance floor—or it would have been if Ram hadn't swept her off her feet and deposited her in the middle of the floor. 'No escaping now,' he told her with a grin.

In Mia's opinion, men who could both dance and look sexy could be counted on the fingers of one hand, and yet Ram managed to do both with ease. And, was it her imagination, or had the track segued into a slower number? And how did she come to be in his arms? Was he making signals to the DJ behind her back? She wouldn't put anything past him.

As the palm of Ram's hand coasted slowly down her back Mia finally had to admit that she had no defences left. Ram must feel her trembling beneath her fine silk dress. And yes, she wanted him. She ached for him. But she held herself away from his seductive heat—until it struck her that, like all those years ago, this could be a charity turn around the floor. Ram had stepped in once before so she didn't feel embarrassed. 'You don't have to do this.'

'What if I want to?'

'What if I know you don't?'

Ram's brow creased attractively. 'I'd have to say you don't know what you're talking about—and I can only assume that all these excuses are to cover for the fact that you're scared of dancing with me.'

'Scared of you?' she huffed.

'If that's not the case then you have nothing to worry about, do you?' he said, dragging her close.

She had plenty to worry about, Mia realised as Ram's heat invaded her body.

'You're doing me a favour, actually,' he confided.

'I am?'

When would she learn not to fall for it? Mia wondered as Ram's lips curved with amusement. 'Who else would dance with me?' he said.

Judging by the envious glances she was attracting—every woman in the club?

'What are you thinking?' Ram demanded when she fell quiet at the thought of so much top-class competition.

Right this moment? No ego-stroking required. But she had an ace up her sleeve. 'I was just wondering if you can tango, actually.'

'Don't push me,' Ram warned.

She would never learn. At a signal from Ram to the DJ the music changed again.

The tango might be the one thing Mia had learned at her starchy all-girls school that came in useful now, but she hadn't factored into her thinking Ram's advanced technique. 'Is there anything you can't do?' she demanded as he bent her low over his arm before yanking her into intimate contact with every hot-wired contour of his body.

She might have known Ram would dance the tango like a gaucho—all brutal control and persuasive seduction, while she had no option but to wrap herself around him—those were simply the demands of the dance.

A circle soon cleared around them. They moved as if they were joined at the hip, staring at each other, intent and un-blinking, as if they would find the meaning of life hidden in each other's eyes. Ram understood the workings of her body better than she did, Mia discovered, and she wasn't the only one to have noticed this. A blur of hungry female eyes only proved that Ram could turn any club steamy. He had set this one on fire the moment he had arrived—and now it was a raging inferno.

And fun. The humour in Ram's stare made the moment theirs—even if everyone else was swept up in an erotic haze. Outwardly, they were putting on a show to scandalise, but this was really an intensely private and fun-filled moment—though

Mia suspected that neither she nor Ram could have guessed quite how well they would move together, or what a blaze of lust-filled heat they could create.

When the music ended everyone applauded as they returned to their seats. 'Wow,' she exclaimed as the electricity between them subsided. 'Where did you learn to dance like that?'

'I could ask the same question of you,' he said.

'I'm afraid my answer would bore you.'

'Try me.'

Mia pulled a face. 'At school. You?'

'The school of life,' Ram confessed, shooting her his very best bad-boy smile.

'Savage.'

'Bluestocking.'

'Scoundrel.'

'Prig.'

She started laughing as they traded insults. It was a long time since she had felt this good.

'They're playing your song,' Ram pointed out.

'You did fix this,' she accused him as 'My Girl' blasted out over the speakers, but then as Ram threw her a sexy grin she had a moment of doubt. Didn't this just prove the lengths he would go to to soften her up and send her home? Maybe Tom had asked Ram to work his magic and persuade her to return to England.

And was she going to worry about that now? Or was she going to have some fun?

No contest, Mia decided as Ram pulled her to her feet. Just for tonight she was going to forget everything and let herself go.

CHAPTER SEVEN

WHEN they left the club the subject of Ram's boat was playing on Mia's mind. She had told the girls she would never go anywhere near it, but they would be so delighted if she could tell them all about it—and Ram was playing into her hands. He had chosen to walk back via the harbour, but he could turn up any one of the little side streets at any time. She had to come right out and ask him: *Please may I see your yacht?* It wouldn't hurt to play the cute little kid sister one more time.

But as it turned out she was somewhat snippier. 'I might as well know what I'm missing,' she said offhandedly. 'Seeing as your yacht is supposed to be the biggest, flashiest and most vulgar yacht in the harbour.'

'So many compliments,' Ram exclaimed, putting his hand on his heart. 'I hardly know how to deal with them.' Fortunately, he was grinning.

'Come on, show me.' Linking arms, she urged him along.

'So who gave you all this info?'

'Didn't you?' she said, acting bemused.

'Me?'

Ram might well seem confused seeing as it was the girls who had talked of nothing else but Ram's fabulous yacht, warning Mia she mustn't return to the apartment without a truckload of insider information. And for once the girls hadn't been exaggerating. Ram's vessel—modestly named *The Star of Ramprakesh*, was indeed a floating city rather than a mere billionaire's plaything. A helicopter and several small speedboats were comfortably housed on one of its many decks. She had seen many of these gleaming white super-yachts berthed in Monte Carlo, but never one to compare with Ram's waterborne palace. It was more the size of a commercial cruise liner than a boat in private ownership. Spectacular? The two of them were dwarfed by it. She felt like an ant—an ant rapidly being consumed by curiosity. 'Can we go on board?'

Ram drew back his head in mock-shock as he grinned down at her. 'Minimal Mia craving a hit of high living? Whatever next?'

'You can stop raising your eyebrows right now, rich boy. Just take me on board.'

She was still on a high from their unexpected rapport at the club, and nothing felt too far out of reach for her now—not even Ram.

Except she should have known better, Mia concluded, feeling the first stirrings of unease as Ram escorted her onboard with the words, 'Welcome to Ramprakesh...'

But when had she ever played it safe? 'So, show me round,' she prompted, surprised at how many crew there were to salute Ram—and how many attendants greeted him with a bow. 'There has to be more to this floating caravan of yours than a dance floor beneath the stars, a ballroom-sized saloon... and a swimming pool?' Mia's eyes widened as she stared in disbelief at the full-sized pool.

'I have to get my exercise somewhere,' Ram explained tongue in cheek. 'And don't forget the cinema, the badminton court, and the practice tee.'

'Show off.'

'Champagne?'

'Oh, I think so.' She felt light-headed—dizzy with excitement. It was all so...magical. And was there any better time to throw caution to the wind than when you knew you were completely safe?

Didn't she always avoid the reality of a situation if her fantasies could create something more appealing?

Shaking off the warning voice, Mia gazed around. There was no doubt that Ram was the supreme ruler of this floating city.

Correct. Nice to see you caught up eventually. Who would know if you disappeared here?

A shiver that warned of change shot down Mia's spine as Ram finished talking to one of the stewards. But Ram would never take advantage of her—and how often did a chance like this come around? She'd asked to come here. Ram had hardly forced her.

And so she was going to chill out and enjoy it. It wouldn't be long before Ram would be sailing out of her life for good—and before he did she wanted to make the most of their time together.

'Ready to see some more?' he said.

'You bet.'

Ram led her across the wide expanse of deck with its comfortable seating areas and occasional tables, and in through some impressive doors into an opulently decorated saloon—which was quite a bit larger than the apartment she shared with the girls. And while she stood gaping Ram opened the glass roof over their heads with a flick of a controller.

'As man toys go, I have to say, that is impressive.'

'Do you like it?' Ram gestured around. 'I had it installed recently. Why don't you give me your professional opinion of the décor, Mia?'

This suggestion both surprised and flattered her. It had been so long since anyone had asked her opinion about design—but then she hadn't exactly broadcast the fact that interior design was her passion after the accident; there had seemed so little point. And while Ram seemed to be asking her a simple question she hadn't missed the hint of challenge in his eyes.

'Okay...'

She looked around. The saloon, as she knew the large

drawing room on board a yacht this size was known, was superbly presented, but when she tried to marry up the grandiose décor with Ram's ultra-modern sliding-roof design she hit a wall. Did she like it? Truthfully? It was all a bit old-fashioned for Ram. On the other hand, she didn't want to rock the boat, so to speak, by insulting his in-house designers. She settled for a mealy-mouthed: 'I honestly don't think I could have done a better job for you, Ram.'

'No quirky twists? I'm disappointed in you, Mia…'

And now she felt a pang of regret and wished she had been braver. It was her off-the-wall ideas that had set her apart, she had been told at college. 'Maybe I'd have capitalised on the light a little more—toned down the background to throw the artwork forward—adjusted the lights—'

'Ah, so you would like to make changes,' he said. 'Are you ready for champagne while you think about them? I'm serious about hearing your suggestions, Mia—I'm thinking of doing a refit.'

Of course you are—the furnishings can't be more than a couple of years old—

But Ram was smiling as if he knew he'd sparked something inside her. 'When you're ready to give me your honest opinion,' he said, confirming this, 'just let me know.'

And so she came up with quite a few more ideas that seemed to please him. 'Don't fill the glass,' she said quickly, seeing something in Ram's eyes that made her wonder if she was quite ready for a Ram-sized challenge—there was an awful lot more yacht to see.

'You're surely not going to risk a bottle of my best going flat. You don't have to drink it,' he added, pressing the crystal flute into her hands. 'All I ask is that you taste it.'

'Just one glass, then.' She wanted this time with Ram. She wanted to see how he had changed. She wanted an insight into his life, however small. And after that tango she needed a chance to unwind and cool down. While Ram poured the drinks she gazed around. 'You know this is pretty much perfect, but if you're serious about letting me loose with my ideas I could make a few more suggestions...'

'I want them all.' His gaze was direct as they chinked glasses.

There was more to that request, Mia sensed. People were trying to force Ram into a box that could never hold him. He was too forward thinking—too energetic in every way to be confined by the traditions of the past. 'Then, for what it's worth, you shall have them.'

'That's all I ask...'

Pity. Now she could only remember how it had felt when he held her in his arms when they danced. Dark and dangerous, and utterly irresistible, Ram was a force of nature—

A force to beware of, Mia warned herself. Pulling away, she put some space between them. Walking a little distance away, she stared out of one of the picture windows from where she had a grandstand view of the small, but perfectly formed, diamond-lit wedding-cake-shaped town that was night-time Monte Carlo. Ram followed and stood close to her, but not touching, so that every part of her tingled with anticipation of his touch.

'What's wrong, Mia? You never used to be so—'

'Boring?' she suggested.

'Touchy. I was thinking more...contained? I thought you had started to relax when we were dancing in the club?'

The tug of Ram's lips only made his dark face more attractive. And he was right—she had relaxed at the club. She had been far too relaxed. It was time to get things back on an even keel. 'What would you think of me if I hadn't changed, Ram? It's been a few years since we last saw each other. What would you think if I were still the same wild child you remember?' Mia's mouth slammed shut. Why ask Ram the one question she didn't want him to answer? Whatever she'd done as a child paled in comparison with what she'd done later when she'd been yearning for him. And even now she didn't want to relax and be his friend; she wanted so much more than that—so much that wasn't good for her.

She walked outside onto the deck, hoping the rapidly cooling air would blast some sense into her. The velvet sky was illuminated by a luminous, waxy moon, while in front of her the inky-black ocean rested silent and mysterious beneath its canopy of diamond stars. There wasn't a single cloud in the sky. The inky-blue was as clear as a blank sheet of paper, making it impossible to imagine a storm had ever threatened earlier. Closing her eyes, she inhaled deeply as she lifted her face to the sky. The air smelled fresh and clean, the tang of the ocean salty and alive with life, mixing with—

The spices of the East. Which could only mean Ram was standing directly behind her.

'Shall we lose the champagne?' he suggested, taking the glass from her hand.

Before she could answer she was in his arms and Ram was kissing her.

She'd thought she had been kissed before. She'd thought wrong. Ram's lips were warm and clever, and he was...extremely good at this, Mia registered as her body melted around him like molten honey.

But wasn't it Ram who had told her that no one could play with fire and expect not to get burned? And shouldn't he know when no fire blazed brighter than his?

She made some feeble attempt to push him away and was thankful Ram refused to budge. And so he teased and stroked and kissed until he was right about them not needing any more champagne, because she was drunk on him. He smiled against her mouth when she whimpered with desire. He knew she was on fire for him, but it was Ram who pulled away first. 'You wanted to see round the rest of the ship, didn't you?' he reminded her.

'Did I?'

Of course she did. 'Lead the way.' She had to gather up

her senses from the untidy heap of broken resolutions she'd dropped on the floor.

'Where would you like to start?' Ram prompted.

'The bridge?' It wasn't the first destination that popped into her mind, but it did seem to be by far the safest bet.

'Then we'll start on the bridge,' Ram agreed.

What she really wanted was for Ram to kiss her again—just so she could convince herself she hadn't imagined the whole thing. This was frustration squared—something she was sure Ram was more than aware of. She even found herself wondering the unthinkable—if she had sex with Ram would she really regret it so much?

'I should go home.'

'Should you?' Ram demanded softly. 'So, go,' he said, standing back to allow her free passage to the gangplank.

So much for that particular little fantasy. She glanced at the shore just a few tantalising feet away, and then back again at Ram. 'If that's what you want…?'

'This is what I want.' He yanked her back into his arms. His hold was firm, and his kiss…his kiss was punishing, passionate and bone-melting.

Who would stand a chance against this type of advanced kissing technique? She would just have to postpone disembarkation for now. And as Ram teased her lips apart, leaving her in no doubt as to what he would like to do next, or how very good he'd be at doing it, she realised that postponement might have to suffer a further considerable delay.

'You don't have to see me back to shore,' she managed to gasp when he finally released her. 'I can easily—'

'What?' Ram demanded. 'Call a cab? Ride a bike? Walk home in the dark?' He shook his head.

'I did bring my cab fare.'

Did he have to smile like that?

'You don't play fair,' she complained as he dragged her back into his arms.

'Who said anything about playing fair?' Ram demanded,

nuzzling her neck to prove that his sharp black stubble had some invisible link to some very sensitive parts of her.

'You don't have to do this,' she insisted in a gasp through well-kissed lips. 'You've done your duty—'

'My duty?' Ram laughed as she struggled desperately for self-control. 'There's no duty involved, Mia, this is sheer unadulterated lust.' And then he pressed her back against the ship's rail to prove it with the heat and power of his erection.

'Oh...'

'Exactly,' he said.

'In that case...'

'You're not in such a hurry to leave?' Ram guessed, his lips curving with amusement as he met Mia's startled gaze.

'The urge isn't as bad as it was.' And she was definitely hungry for more. 'I realise I've still got so much to learn—about what you want me to do—with your interior design, I mean...'

She was rambling now and they both knew it. Also, they were both adults—they both wanted this, and she couldn't see why the next few hours shouldn't be very educational indeed. And so she gorged herself on the taste of Ram—fresh, clean and totally irresistible. She even tried to pretend she was in control when his hands moved down her back, but she definitely wasn't herself by the time he cupped her buttocks and rubbed against her. In fact, she was a brazen hussy by then, and as a riot of sensation invaded her body a rush of dreams filled her mind suggesting anything was possible—

And then she staggered against him. 'What's happening?' she demanded, clinging onto Ram for dear life.

'Nothing for you to worry about,' he said as he steadied her. 'I think we just picked up speed—'

'What?' Mia threw a panicky glance over her shoulder. 'What do you mean we've picked up speed?'

'We've cleared the harbour and so we're allowed to go faster.'

'You mean we're going out to sea?' She gazed round wildly, trying to clear the haze in her mind, she'd never even noticed the engines starting up.

'It's quite usual when we leave the harbour.'

'So it's just a short trip—like testing the engines, or something?'

'I think it might be a bit more than that.'

'What do you mean, a bit more?' Her voice was rising to the point where she sounded on the verge of hysteria. But this wasn't a joke. She wasn't a child, and this wasn't one of her childhood fantasies. 'You'd better tell me where we're going,' she said, gathering her wits about her. Shooting an anxious glance at the fast-receding shoreline, she was already calculating how long it would take them to turn around.

'You always loved surprises, Mia.'

Kissing Ram absolutely qualified as an acceptable surprise. Flirting with him? Yes, that too. But being seduced onto his super-yacht with just the promise of a guided tour? How dumb was she? 'Maybe I did used to love surprises but that was half a lifetime ago and you can't just take me anywhere you want without my say-so, Ram.'

'Watch me.'

'Don't be ridiculous—you have to take me back.'

'No,' he said flatly.

'What did you say?'

'Get used to it, Mia. You're coming with me.'

She had underestimated Ram and the ease with which his sophisticated yacht could slip out of harbour—making barely a sound.

CHAPTER EIGHT

HE'D reasoned it this way. He had a duty towards Mia. If it had been his sister holed up in Monte Carlo in a dead-end job—going nowhere, distanced from her family—he knew Tom would have stepped in.

Of course, there was another part of this reasoning that could not include some fictional sister and his brother-in-arms. He was attracted to Mia—intrigued by her too. She had always been different, and now she was all grown-up he wasn't ready to let go of her yet. 'You can yell all you like,' he told her as she swore at him like a trooper. 'No one's listening.'

'So, you're kidnapping me?' she demanded as his sleek white yacht speeded up, leaving the shoreline far behind in its silvery wake.

'Don't you trust me, Mia?'

'Don't you use that look on me, Ram Varindha,' she told him furiously.

He had always wanted Mia to trust him, but since Tom's engagement party Mia had doubted him—doubted his intentions. Well, she needn't doubt them now—they were wholly dishonourable.

'You kissed me so I wouldn't notice the boat leaving dock.'

'I kissed you because I wanted to.'

She touched her lips. 'You wanted to…' She paused for

the briefest moment and then she rounded on him. 'And I'm supposed to believe that?'

Ram had perfected the Look, Mia decided. It was the look she had always wanted to see on his face, but not now—not now when she needed her wits about her.

'Where do you think you're going?' he demanded as she walked away.

She hardly knew herself. 'To make a call—to the authorities,' she said, firming up her plans as she pulled out her phone.

'Why don't you calm down, Mia?' he said, catching up with her in a couple of strides. 'I'm hardly the enemy.' And then he laughed as if this were all one of their childhood jokes. 'Or do you want me to restrain you?' he murmured, bringing her close.

'I don't think that's very funny, Ram…'

But as Ram angled his chin to level a challenging stare at her, her gaze slipped to his lips. 'You wouldn't dare,' she whispered.

Ram's brow lifted, leaving her to battle an intoxicating mix of excitement and erotic terror.

'I've got plenty of time to decide what to do with you,' he promised.

'How long exactly?' she pressed, refusing to be schmoozed. 'Don't you realise I have to go to work tomorrow?'

'I took care of that.'

'What do you mean, you took care of it?' she demanded, losing it again.

'I thought you looked a little jaded.' He curbed a smile. 'Monsieur Michel agreed with me—so we booked some time off for you—'

'We? We booked some time off?' Mia exploded. 'You did *what*? How dare you? You had absolutely no right! You can't make decisions for me.' All the time she was yelling at him a little curl of excitement was busy in her lower regions—not that that was any reason to let Ram off the hook. He'd gone too far this time. 'There are other people who will report me missing,' she told him confidently.

'Your flatmates?'

Of course, he must have spoken to them too, Mia realised, and the girls would only applaud what they would see as Ram's extravagantly romantic gesture. 'You set this whole thing up—you can't deny it.'

'To be fair, it hasn't been long in the planning.'

The breath shot out of her lungs as he yanked her to him. 'Are you sure you want to go back, Mia?'

'Are you sure you know what you've taken on?' she countered, only to spoil the effect of her threat by shivering with uncontrollable lust as Ram brushed her mouth with his lips. 'So, what happens now?' she said, shaking herself round to some semblance of lucidity.

'What would you like to happen?' Ram stroked her arms. 'I could take you back in the helicopter...'

And just when she should have said: *Yes, you do that*—she hesitated.

'You used to love adventures, Mia.'

'Yes. When I was in control of them.'

'You're in control now,' Ram assured her. His grip softened in a way that made her want the moment to last forever. 'I'll take you back if that's what you really want...'

A frown brewed inside her. Was that what she really wanted? Or was this...?

'Stay or go, make your mind up,' Ram pointed out.

'I'd like to...'

'What?' he murmured. 'What would you like, Mia?'

She wanted to be with Ram. She wanted to be his equal— if not in wealth and status, then at least in determination to fulfil her potential. Monsieur Michel had taken a chance on her and she hadn't let him down. Maybe she could pick up her design career. Her girlfriends had never mentioned her injuries—Ram hardly seemed to notice them. Maybe she was just too wrapped up in herself—maybe she needed to take this opportunity Ram was offering her and exploit it on every level. She wanted him, didn't she? She wanted to take the stuffy life he seemed happy to return to and turn it on its head. Suddenly all this burst out as, 'I'd like to build rather than coast along—I'd like to pick up my life, Ram.'

He went still and she fell silent, feeling rather foolish now. But she hadn't finished yet. She couldn't leave it here and braced herself for what had to come next. 'So we take this trip together. What then?' As Ram loosened his grip on her she felt as vulnerable as she ever had. There were no false promises in his eyes, or glib words falling from his lips. There was just the usual steel-trap brain working through the possibilities.

'I could arrange an introduction to my design team—if that's what you want?'

Of course his thoughts would all be practical. There could be no talk of love and marriage, horse and carriage. 'That's very generous of you, Ram.' And she meant it. How many people had taken a chance on her? Maybe it was time to pick herself up, she'd raced again—she could take back the rest of her dreams.

'We might even be able to involve you in one of the new projects.'

Oh, he knew just how to work her. But there was no harm in finding out more. 'I'm listening…'

'Let's go inside.'

The decision was made, Mia realised as they turned their back on the sea. Ram had baited the trap and she had walked in happily—but there was more than a piece of cheese at stake here. Ram was a practised seducer, while she had a heart so full of holes thanks to him it was like a sieve. 'Will you let me off at the next port?'

'You could hop off when we reach the Suez Canal, I suppose.'

Mia's mouth formed a question, but no sound came out, and before she could demand an explanation, Ram said coolly, 'Perhaps you'd better sleep on it—let's talk tomorrow. There's plenty of time, Mia,' he added when she looked at him blankly. 'This won't be a short voyage. I'll have one of the stewards show you to your suite of rooms—'

'My suite of rooms? So you knew I'd stay?'

Of course he had. Ram wasn't noted for his careless gestures—more for his exploits in the business world and the bedroom, which he executed with the same icy precision. And she had briefly thought he was the same easy-going childhood friend? A lot had happened to Ram since then—things she didn't know about or understand.

That ice pick was bounding off his heart again, Mia mused as Ram walked away. So much for banishing the nightmares—'Ram—wait—'

'I have things to do, Mia.'

He didn't even break stride. He just called back to her over his shoulder and kept right on walking.

'Stay, Mia.'

'What do you think I am—a dog?'

'I'll send the steward.'

She gave chase. 'What *things* do you have to do, Ram? You were ready to take me back to shore in the helicopter a moment ago.'

'Yes, I was, but you made that unnecessary—and now it's too late.'

She hung on to his arm like a terrier to a bone. 'The least you can do is talk to me—tell me where we're going.'

'I'm taking you somewhere you always wanted to go.'

Ramprakesh?

'Tell me,' Mia insisted as the land of her dreams took shape in her mind. Ram's homeland had always conjured up images of palaces and fireworks and elephants—and hellishly good-looking princes called Ram—

By this time Ram was halfway down the stairs and she surprised herself with just how fast she could fly down a flight of stairs. 'Why?' she demanded, leaping ahead of him. 'Why have you done all this?'

'Because the time is right and because I might need you again.'

She didn't like the sound of that. 'So you think I might be *useful* to you?' The kiss must have been a try-out that left him cold—a ruse to distract her while the yacht slipped out of its berth. And that hurt.

'Being useful is bad?' he said, lips pressing down as if he couldn't work that one out.

'No. It isn't bad—but when you want someone to do something for you, it's usual to ask them first rather than assume they'll fall into line.'

He thought about that for a nanosecond. 'No time,' he said. 'Some things just have to be executed and then discussed later.'

'I'm not a thing, Ram.'

His brows rose as if he were surprised at that.

She gave up. 'You're impossible.'

'So I've been told,' he agreed. 'But I am serious about having a design job I think you might be interested in—and you could start by taking a look around this overstuffed wedding cake—'

'You don't like the décor on the yacht?'

'What do you think?'

There was still a glimmer of the old Ram there. No reason to go easy on him, though. 'You didn't have to kidnap me to get my thoughts on your yacht.'

'I'll ignore the dramatic flourish. Firstly, I didn't kidnap you—you came onboard of your own accord. And secondly, you can of course sulk for the entire voyage, but I wouldn't recommend it.'

Mia ground her jaw. It had been too long since she had played this type of mind game with Ram—she was a little rusty. But Ram *and* Ramprakesh—not to mention that promise to meet with his design team. Was she going to cut off her nose to spite her face and give the plastic surgeon another headache? 'I'll do it,' she agreed. 'I'll take a look round your yacht—but only on my terms.'

'Which are?'

'You treat me with respect and pay the going rate—as an interior designer,' she added hurriedly before he could get any other ideas. 'I'll look at the project first and then I'll decide if I want to become involved.'

'Okay.'

Okay? That was it? Mia blinked. But then her mind cleared and she realised that back in Monte Carlo Ram had asked her why her design career had gone up in smoke, and instead of making fun of her for losing her confidence he had done this. And as much as she wanted to yell at him for manipulating her, she couldn't help but be a little bit thrilled that life and Ram had finally given her the challenge she had been looking for. This might even work out—just so long as she kept everything in proportion and accepted this was Ram helping a childhood friend out of a hole and nothing more.

So, her decision was made—there was nothing to stop her dipping her toe in the water—

Her toe? Heck, this was full naked-body immersion, Mia realised, seeing Ram's lips tug with satisfaction as he walked away. She only had to touch her own lips and feel how swollen they were to know how far out of her depth she was. Ram was certainly determined to take her on a voyage of discovery.

But he was also giving her the chance to pick up the pieces of the career she had loved...

'Mademoiselle?' A steward dressed in immaculate whites distracted her. 'May I show you to your quarters, *mademoiselle*?'

Why not? In for a penny, in for a few billion pounds... 'Thank you,' she said, smiling wryly as he led the way.

Oh, this was fabulous.

How easily she was bought, Mia reflected as she followed the steward down one gilt-bedecked corridor after another.

But, although the decoration was vibrant and luxurious, it was all a bit over the top. She could see why Ram had fed her the bait. His yacht was huge and equipped with all the latest high-tech equipment, but the interior design was more suitable for his parents' generation. If he was serious about combining stewardship of a country with his business interests, then Ram needed to showcase not just his country's traditional wares, but the latest innovations too. Given half a chance she would encourage new young Ramprakeshi designers to submit their products for his consideration.

Oh, how she wanted this brief, Mia mused, soaking in every bit of information she could as she looked around. She had never seen so many priceless artefacts and paintings outside a museum, and it came home to her then that, although everyone thought they knew Ram, few had seen him as she had—relaxed, approachable, humorous, sexy. They just saw what he was worth and drew their own conclusions about what he would want around him.

Ram hadn't just come back into her world; he'd turned that world on its axis, Mia realised. And as for The Kiss... kisses, kissing... She touched her eyepatch. However brave she appeared there was always part of her that thought people—especially men—found her injuries off-putting, but not only had Ram proved that wasn't the case as far as he was concerned, but he didn't make allowances for them either, which she liked. She didn't want to be treated like an invalid, or an object of pity. So for all the black strikes against him, he had earned quite a few brownie points too.

'Am I alone on this corridor?' she asked as the steward stopped by one particular door. It was too much to hope Ram would be next door—and, of course, she didn't want that anyway. She was just...well—getting her bearings.

'The master has a suite of rooms on another level, *mademoiselle.*'

'Up or down?'

'Directly behind the bridge, *mademoiselle.*'

Okay, so not that close. She breathed a sigh of relief.

As the steward held the door open she completely forgot how mad Ram could make her. The accommodation she had been allocated took her breath away. This was luxury on an unprecedented scale.

'There's more, *mademoiselle*,' the steward prompted her as she stood gaping at the door.

'More?' She sounded like a child at Christmas, hardly knowing which gift to open first. Forget the granny curtains and the quilted shiny satin throws—there were floor-to-ceiling windows and enough space to fit three apartments the same size as the one she shared with the girls. And at least the bed, with its silken drapes, tented canopy, tassels, fringes and assorted twinkles, boasted crisp white linen sheets, and a most inviting bank of pillows...

She touched her lips—still swollen...still tingling with the memory of Ram's kisses...

'Would you like me to show you round, *mademoiselle*?'

She started guiltily as the steward coughed politely. 'Yes, please,' she managed faintly, dragging her gaze away from the emperor-sized bed.

The furniture was all hand-carved and polished with precious inlays of ebony and semi-precious stones—and, as she'd thought, the steward confirmed that the handles had all been cast in solid gold. 'Oh, yes, very nice,' she said politely, thinking Ram would prefer something funky and that most of these things should be in a museum.

'Would you like me to show you the rest of the suite, *mademoiselle*...?'

'I'll find my way around, thank you' she said with a smile. She was dying to be alone to do some serious thinking, but first there was more investigating to do...

There was a pink marble bathroom where a bleached blonde Barbie doll would be right at home—and a fully fitted dressing room that would fulfil the dreams of the most impossibly spoiled celebrity. The square bath was big enough for four. And as for the walk-in drench shower…

Well, that was definitely big enough for…

Activities, Mia decided, poking her head around the corner to size it up. Activities she could only dream about indulging in with Ram—

Activities she definitely wouldn't be indulging in, Mia informed herself firmly.

Unfortunately, that self-imposed ban wasn't enough to stop her imagination conjuring up a few heart-stopping scenes. To stop them dead she turned full circle slowly, concentrating her mind solely on her thoughts as an interior designer—Ram had switched a light on in her brain, and now she found it impossible to look at a single object or paint shade without giving it a professional review.

She had Ram to thank for throwing her back into that world of breaking boundaries and thinking outside the box. Nothing about this visit was accidental, Mia concluded. Ram knew her life before the accident had drawn its oxygen from design, but she mustn't mistake his concern for anything else.

There were some things she would like to keep—this crimson, tangerine and fuchsia decoration in the dining room, for instance, where the colours had been allowed to clash in such a strange and fabulous way. This was a whole new language of design, and one she could use to embellish her contemporary take on things. Opening the sliding glass door, she moved outside onto the balcony with its wooden decking. It was still quite warm outside. Looking back into the dining room, she knew it would be flooded with light in the morning, but she would prefer to eat breakfast out here, and dream about Ram—

'Ram!' He was standing in the doorway, dangling a set of keys. Ram—fresh from the shower with his hair still damp, dressed in snug-fitting jeans with sexy bare feet and a crisp, clean shirt with the sleeves pushed back to reveal his powerful forearms.

'This is your last chance,' he threatened, giving the keys a little shake.

'Haven't we gone too far for you to take me back?'

'I could drop you off in Italy.'

'I suppose you think that's funny?' She firmed her jaw. 'As much as it tempts me to have you at my beck and call, Ram Varindha, I'm going to resist the temptation to put your flying abilities to the test—so you can put those keys away for now.'

'Mia, Mia, Mia. You know you don't want to give me that sort of test.'

'I have no idea what you mean,' she assured him, wondering if it was possible for a body to melt like candle wax—which was what hers seemed to be doing.

Ram moved so fast she was in his arms before she had chance to think. 'You're just so—'

'Arrogant and impossible?' he suggested with a husky laugh.

'That's nothing to be proud of,' she said, thinking red-hot, rich and royal didn't even begin to describe him. And Ram was most definitely used to getting his own way. It was about time she threw out a few challenges of her own. 'Do you always go flying with bare feet?'

'That depends on how high I'm planning to take you.'

By the time she had processed that piece of information Ram was kissing her.

CHAPTER NINE

'You seemed a little surprised to see me?' Ram observed, cupping Mia's face to stare at her intently.

'I thought you had things to do.'

'I do. And you're top of my list—'

'Ram—'

'You can't act shocked when your nipples are drilling a hole through my shirt.'

'Always the romantic.'

'No, that's you.'

'You're really bad,' Mia gasped as he attacked her neck with tantalising kisses.

'And would you have me any other way?'

'Do I get a choice?' Her lips felt swollen; other parts of her too. Her eyes had to be black as night. She was all sensation…all hunger and fear and lust and uncertainty. What did she know about sex other than some random fumbling with boys as gauche and inexperienced as she was?

And Ram was a master of the erotic arts, as he was proving without too much effort, so why was she worried?

Was it usual for two people to fit together so well when there was such a difference in their size? She pressed herself against him—just to confirm she wasn't mistaken. And sighed as sensation ripped through her body.

'You like that?' Ram said, moving against her until she couldn't think straight.

'I'm surprised you can find the time for it,' she gasped, clinging by her fingertips to what remained of her sanity.

'I can always find time for you, Mia…'

'Oh…' The waves of pleasure were coming thick and fast now, clouding her mind—or what remained of it. All she wanted to do was relish the sensitivity in Ram's fingertips as he ran them down her spine, and snuggle as close as she could into his warm, muscular body…

But she had to remember Ram had spirited her away from Monte Carlo on this mystery voyage without so much as asking her permission. 'You're lucky I'm as calm as I am,' she managed shakily, at which Ram's lips pressed down with amusement.

'I thought you might have noticed by now that I use very particular calming techniques.'

'I did notice.' Maybe if she weren't quite so receptive to Ram's touch she might be able to get her head round what was happening. Ram kissing her; Ram wanting her; Ram making love to her—

'I'd hate to overstay my welcome,' he said.

She blinked. Was he offering to leave? 'You could stay and make amends,' she countered on a wave of desire.

'Make amends how?' Ram demanded huskily, brushing her swollen mouth with his lips.

'I'm sure I'll think of something.'

'I'm sure you will,' he agreed.

'Don't sound so confident,' she warned him. 'I'm still angry with you—furious, actually.'

'Oh, no.' Ram pretended concern. 'What can I do to make things right?'

'This time you must come up with a solution,' she informed him. 'I can't think of anything you could do to make up for your bad behaviour.' *Except kiss me again…and again and again…*

'I think I'm going to make you wait—'

'What?' she exclaimed as he moved away.

'Restraint is good for you.'

'Not in this instance.' It had left her with an unholy ache.

'Oh, and if you don't like the accommodation I've chosen for you,' Ram said as if he hadn't heard her, 'I can always have someone show you round the yacht and you can choose a suite of rooms more to your liking.'

Knowing her luck she'd choose his. 'I'm fine here, thank you. In fact, I think I'd like to take a shower now.' She glanced pointedly at the door. Ram couldn't have it all his own way.

'A shower? That's a good idea. Why don't I lend a hand?'

'Ram, I'm warning you...'

As if he were going to pay any heed. 'Put me down. I can bathe myself.'

'That's no fun.'

'Put...Me...Down...This...Minute.'

He did—but on the bed.

'It seems I have some serious apologising to do.'

'You certainly do,' Mia agreed. If this was nothing more than a frustration-induced fantasy she was with it all the way.

'Maybe we should leave this for another time?' Ram suggested, his rich voice dark and teasing.

'Maybe we should.' Reaching up, she tested her hands on the corded muscles of his upper arms, closing her fingers slowly, yet firmly, to keep him close. 'But I don't want to.'

'You don't?' Ram's kisses lit a burning trail towards her mouth.

'Oh, Ram, I want you...so much...'

There was nothing like keeping him guessing.

'Don't make me wait,' she warned him for good measure.

But Ram took his time undressing her. He understood all about delay. She knew nothing and was just happy to learn.

The slip of a dress fell away and she was naked to the waist underneath it. Her nipples were bright pink and engorged, and even her breasts seemed fuller. Ram seemed to approve, judging by the way he was stroking them…moulding them… weighing them appreciatively with his hands, and generally teasing her senses to a point where she was writhing unashamedly on the bed and making uncharacteristic little whimpering sounds.

With each delicate rasp of his nails on the tips of her nipples she felt a corresponding urge to arc her body towards him. She did have everything to learn. It was as if there were an invisible connection between her nipples and other parts of her that were swelling rapidly as if to catch Ram's attention— parts that were moistly preparing for his most thorough and prolonged attention. Just a slip of lace separated them now, though Ram was still full clothed…

'Is this fair?' she demanded, reaching for the buttons on his shirt.

'Do your worst,' he challenged, throwing his head back so she saw his full potential, from the thickly corded column of his neck, to the impossibly wide spread of his shoulders and his powerful chest. She needed no further encouragement. The hunger to feel Ram's hot, hard flesh against her was the only thought in her head now, and so she ripped at his shirt, tugging it out of his jeans and yanking it over his head, registering a wealth of muscles on the way. 'You're beautiful,' she exclaimed.

'Stop stealing my lines,' Ram said, laughing.

She watched his hands in fascination as he undid the buckle on his belt. Snatching it out of his grasp, she snapped it through the loops on his jeans and tossed it aside, returning immediately to relieve the emergency situation swiftly building beneath the tightly packed denim. *Oh, my G—*

Was she ready for this?

Steady. She was taking this too fast—giving Ram the wrong idea. If he impaled her on him without proper preparation she'd be damaged for life.

'Scared?' he asked. And when she mumbled something

unintelligible, he added, 'I understand. A little healthy respect for the sex act is always a good thing.'

'The sex act,' she repeated, snatching at anything now to delay the inevitable. 'Can't we make love? Or maybe start with a cuddle?'

'Relax and enjoy,' Ram murmured, easing his jeans over his hips. 'We're in no hurry. Just listen to your body as I touch you…'

Her body was singing an opera with a cast of thousands and didn't seem to know how to turn the volume down. And now Ram was naked and the brush of his hot flesh against her body was a tantalising hint of what she could expect. His control reassured her. She wouldn't have trusted herself to be so restrained. And all that strength married with control was more aphrodisiac than she could handle. And to think it was all at her service…

Ram's powerful hands could deliver the most delicate of touches. His long, lean fingers were precision-engineered instruments of pleasure. And then there were his kisses, long and lingering—in the sensitive crook of her elbow, down her neck and across her chest, until finally, gloriously, they reached her breasts, and then her belly and now her inner thighs…

She was so swollen and moist by the time he touched her she barely left him anything else to do. Or so she thought until Ram moved down the bed and eased her legs over his shoulders, when she learned she was wrong about that too. And how did he play her that way—bringing her to the edge and knowing just when to pull back?

By the time he moved over her she had forgotten her fears and welcomed him with no inhibitions, drawing her knees back as he claimed her to her own soundtrack of sighs and sobs as she grasped at him frantically, clutching him close as he moved to take her completely.

When she was sure she couldn't bear any more pleasure he began to move, slowly at first, and then with increasing speed and resolve until she was wild for him and wild for the ending they both knew could only be a heartbeat away.

'How am I going to cool you down?' Ram demanded when hours had passed in a hazy mist of pleasure.

Daylight might have faded, but her appetite for Ram was still intact, Mia discovered. 'Are you complaining?' she demanded softly. 'Am I too much for you, perhaps?'

'Too much for me?' Ram grinned. 'You don't know me at all.'

Unfortunately, that was true, Mia reflected. They had gone about this back to front, starting with intimate before they even knew what made each other tick—except here in bed, of course.

Ram covered her hand with his when she reached for him. 'There's nothing I love more than a strong woman who knows what she wants,' he said. 'Especially one that's badly in need of cooling down.' And hoisting her over his shoulder, he headed for the bathroom.

'You wouldn't,' she screamed with excitement when he turned the shower on cold.

'Really?' he said mildly, and the next thing she knew she was under it, screaming her lungs out as the icy water thundered down.

'I'll never forgive you for this.'

'Until I warm you up again,' Ram guessed.

He guessed correctly.

'You are so going to pay,' Mia exclaimed, dragging Ram beneath the shower with her.

In a heartbeat they were wrestling with Mia's main aim being to wrap her rapidly cooling body around Ram's red-hot frame.

'Make me pay, baby.'

She laughed incredulously. 'Have you no shame?'

'None,' Ram confirmed.

There was only one small fly in this seductive ointment. If life had taught her anything it was that she couldn't have everything she wanted, and that what seemed to be the most precious to her was always the one thing that got away—

'Penny for them,' Ram demanded, catching her close so he could tease her with kisses.

'I want you again.' And she wanted to keep those other thoughts away.

'Oh, you do…' He pinned her firmly against the wall. 'Had I better take the edge off?'

'If you think that's all you can manage.'

Ram's eyes burned with the confidence she loved. 'I'll just have to do the best I can,' he said.

'And that will have to be enough for me, I suppose,' Mia teased right back.

'Give me some directions here—is this what you want?'

'Getting there,' she conceded, locking her legs around his waist.

But she wanted more than to just take the edge off her physical hunger—she wanted everything Ram had to give and more, Mia realised, wishing she could lose herself in pleasure and forget about the unlikelihood of anything long-term developing between them.

'Like this?' Ram murmured.

She sank gratefully into his erotic world. 'It's a start,' she gasped, leaning back in his arms.

'Perhaps I'll allow you a little bit more, then,' he said, sinking fractionally deeper like a miser eking out his treasure.

She angled her body shamelessly. 'I want more—I want it all.'

'You're a very greedy girl,' Ram said, withdrawing fractionally. 'What's your hurry?' he breathed against her throat. 'We've got all the time in the world.'

Had they?

'You promised to heat me up,' she reminded him, suddenly conscious again of the freezing shower.

'And I never break a promise,' he agreed.

He entered her slowly, taking his time to appreciate every

hot muscle Mia closed so greedily around him. 'Are you sure this is what you want?' he teased her as she whimpered.

'If it isn't you're in serious trouble,' she promised, arcing towards him.

She groaned with pleasure as he took her deep. 'Like this?' he suggested.

'Exactly like that,' she confirmed, dragging in a gasping breath. 'Except you're not allowed to stop.'

'What, never?'

'I'll tell you when.'

He laughed and shook his hair out of his eyes. 'Message received and understood,' he assured her, moving just the way she liked. 'I could probably talk you over the edge.'

'You probably could—but what fun would that be?' she demanded, rocking with him. 'And I don't want you getting lazy just when I've got you trained.'

'You've got *me* trained?' But he couldn't resist and so he thrust her over the edge just for the pleasure of hearing her scream. 'Now who's in control?' he murmured as he soothed her down.

'You are,' she whispered. 'That's the good thing about training—it massively improves a man's control.'

'Not any man,' he said.

Maybe it was the tone of his voice—or maybe the extremes of cold outside and hot inside—but she snapped alert and stared at him. 'Only one man can do what you can—at least where I'm concerned.' And then she laughed to cover for the suddenly serious tone of her voice.

'What?' he said.

'You should have warned me we were going to indulge in extreme sports—I'd have taken out travel insurance.'

'I'll take care of you,' Ram said, realising he meant it. 'But don't for one moment think the training is all one-sided, or that it's almost over.' He turned the shower to warm and lowered her carefully onto the marble floor.

'Where are you taking me?' Mia demanded as he swung her into his arms.

'Back to bed,' he said. 'Unless you can think of a better place?'

For once, it seemed he had hit upon an argument with which even Mia couldn't disagree. He carried her into the bedroom, grabbing a towel on the way, while Mia kept her legs locked round his waist and her hands firmly clamped on his shoulders.

'I'm not going anywhere,' he reassured her as they continued their crazy journey across the floor.

'You're right about that,' she said, tightening her hold on him as he tipped her backwards onto the bed.

'Now,' she commanded.

'Is this any way for a lady to behave?'

'I'm not a lady, I'm a pirate queen—and they used to keep harems of men for their pleasure.'

'No harems,' he warned.

'Then you have to do the work of twenty men.'

'So, I'm your sex slave now?'

'Call it anyway you want—but if you must talk, do it later.'

They both started to laugh as he stared down at her while holding himself on braced arms a teasing inch away.

'Well?' she said. 'What are you waiting for?'

He was just thinking how lovely she was—and how lucky he was.

'Be gentle with me,' she teased him, writhing on the bed. 'I'm so much smaller than you are.'

'Like I haven't noticed that.'

'You wouldn't?' she said, when he took her wrists in a loose grip, holding them above her head on the bank of pillows.

'You're right,' he said. 'I wouldn't.' He released her, making her reach for him, and then found himself kissing teardrops from her cheek. When he asked her about them she laughed and said she must be allergic to him, and when he narrowed his eyes she told him to get over it, she had—and so he let it go.

She couldn't let Ram get to her. He was doing what he did best, while this was so much more for her. She must not fall in love with him. He would know immediately and then he'd pull away. And if he left her life a second time, she couldn't bear it.

'I think we should start over—and without the tears this time, Mia.'

She had no argument with that. 'As many times as you have strength for,' she agreed.

'It's going to be a long night,' Ram promised.

CHAPTER TEN

MIA woke to find her body aching pleasantly, and she was all neatly tucked up in bed.

Ram's doing, she suspected immediately.

She stretched, revelling in the scent of clean sheets overlaid with Ram's delicious scent. The extraordinary events of the previous day came back to her like the most wonderful dream, but when she turned to look for Ram there was no sign of him.

He'd let her sleep. So she'd take a shower and then place a call…

The receptionist on board put Mia straight through to Ram. 'Hey, bad boy,' she said, feeling all warm inside. 'What am I supposed to wear? I only have one dress with me—and that's looking a bit…shall we say, manhandled.' The coral slip dress was still lying where Ram had tossed it.

'Only one dress?' he said in surprise.

'This isn't a joke, Ram. I can't wear a towel round the ship.'

'But I might like that.'

'Seriously,' she warned.

'Okay,' he murmured, speaking in an intimate tone, 'I'll set you a challenge. How many wardrobes can you find in the dressing room?'

'I don't know,' Mia said impatiently, already wriggling off the bed.

'It's not like you to be so slow off the mark.'

She was already at the door. 'You are in so much trouble, Ram Varindha.'

'I like the sound of that.'

'You did plan this,' she said, flinging back door after wardrobe door. They were packed with the most delectable clothes.

'I never know when I'm going to have guests,' Ram told her.

'Enough,' she yelled back. 'If you think I want to hear about the women who pass through here—'

'It's a brand-new yacht, Mia.'

'So the fact that I'm the first of many is supposed to make me feel better?'

'You'd be doing me a favour if you'd sample the selection.'

Ram was laughing as he cut the line.

Her intention had been to take a moment to calm down—but what actually happened was that she conducted a thorough search of every drawer and cupboard, and she wasn't disappointed. Whatever she might think of the interior design on board Ram's yacht, whoever had stocked the dressing room knew exactly what they were doing—but there were more outfits here than she could possibly wear...

Sinking down onto the sofa, she tried to get her head around what she'd found, and it was then her attention was drawn to the artwork on the walls. It was a series of paintings that told a story—a love story—an erotic love story—

The shrill chirrup of the phone jerked her out of her contemplations. 'Did you find something to wear?' Ram demanded.

'Yes,' she said distractedly, her gaze still fixed on the pictures on the walls.

'Well, are you coming to show me?'

'Yes,' she said briefly, putting the phone down. The first

painting showed two lovers reclining on silken cushions as they fed each other grapes. The colours were glorious, and like the others the painting had the most beautiful brushwork, but as she looked along the row she realised there was a hidden meaning in each of them. The message came over loud and clear—eating was just one sensory pleasure, but there were many more. In fact, there were quite a few she had never heard of before—

The next image showed the same two lovers, but now their clothes were sliding off their polished shoulders as they gazed into each other's eyes beneath a purple sky. The lovers were beautifully drawn and their clothes were ravishing—flowing silks in vibrant orange and brightest pink, with turquoise-blue and gold decoration. The girl was kneeling with her arms resting loosely on the man's shoulders—

Understanding trickled into Mia's brain with all the speed of congealed honey forcing its way through the opening of a pipette. This wasn't simply a stateroom, it was a collecting pen for a harem—and Ram was no longer simply her extremely accomplished lover, but a collector of living, breathing arte-facts, which he kept alongside his inanimate collectables. And while this might intrigue and even arouse her in some dark and forbidden way, she had no intention of signing up for a team.

But she was here. And this was a fairy-tale set-up. Perhaps if she kept her head she could keep her pride too *and* ex-perience something very special And there were the most breathtaking outfits in the wardrobes—a rainbow assortment of floating chiffon, clingy tissue-crêpe and lightweight silk.

Temptation overwhelmed her. The fact that they were tra-ditional Ramprakeshi clothes only made the dress-up urge that much stronger.

She'd keep it plain, Mia decided, choosing the simplest outfit she could find. Modest, with a twist, was how she would describe it. She was going to start the way she meant to go on, which meant most decidedly *not* as one of the Maharajah's many concubines.

Guessing she might need some help arranging a sari correctly for the first time, she chose to wear a *salwar-kameez* suit. The *kameez* was a loose shirt with long sleeves, and the lightweight *salwar* pants were flattering. She started out choosing a pale peach outfit trimmed with pearls—it was exquisite. But then she changed her mind and gravitated towards a strong cobalt blue that picked up the colour of her good eye. Jewelled beads in a deeper shade of blue decorated the deeply slashed neckline as well as the edges of the cuffs, and there was a matching scarf with beaded tassel fringing that glittered seductively in the subdued lighting as she arranged it around her neck. There was nothing subtle about it, but if she was going to take up Ram's challenge to stay on board and keep hold of her pride there could be no half measures—

As if there ever could be such a thing as half measures with Ram.

But should she be going to quite so much trouble with her appearance if she was only one of a crowd?

Yes, Mia argued with her boringly sensible inner voice. Ram would take any sloppiness on her part as a sign of weakness, and she was going to leave this floating pleasure palace with her head held high.

This was a very different look for her, Mia conceded, examining her reflection in the mirror. With her hair freshly washed and curling softly together with the flattering clothes, she looked quite feminine. For the first time since the accident she opened her make-up bag and lined both her eyes with kohl. The effect was startling. Even her damaged eye looked reasonably okay.

She was almost prepared to go commando in that respect and had left her eyepatch on the shelf. She was feeling positive right up to the moment when she slipped on a pair of jewelled sandals that had clearly been handmade to tone with the suit.

She was perched on the edge of the bed admiring them… admiring the fit—

Springing up, she quickly realised that this wasn't a variety of clothes for a variety of guests young and old—or even for a selection of women of all sizes, as she had first suspected—but a very particular collection to suit and fit a particular woman. Every single piece of clothing and pair of shoes was in her size.

A thrill of triumph and relief rushed through her at the thought of all those phantom women—defeated without a blow being struck—and another that Ram had done this for her. But that didn't let him off the hook. He'd made some pretty nifty moves to get all this in place in the short span of time from their first meeting at Monsieur Michel's salon to his boat slipping out of the harbour. And yes, money could buy most things and have them delivered to your door—but not her.

Stormy weather? Mia secured her eyepatch in place. Ram had better batten down the hatches; there was a hurricane on the way.

She looked like a fallen angel swooping down on him. When Mia stormed into the saloon to confront him he knew exactly what was on her mind. That was the trouble—they knew each other instinctively, but they had yet to get to know each other on a more everyday level.

He guessed Mia had been working up this tantrum out on deck—she was windswept. Her eyes were dark with passion, and her hair framed her angry face like a thunder cloud.

She stopped dead in her tracks when she saw him comfortably seated on the sofa. 'Come in,' he said as if all was well with the world. 'Sit down,' he invited politely, indicating the sofa facing his. 'You look—'

'Nice?' she interrupted.

'I was about to say—a little tense—'

'A little tense?' she roared at him. 'I know you planned

SAVE OVER £39

25% OFF

Sign up to get 4 stories a month for 12 months in advance and **SAVE £39.60** – that's a fantastic 25% off
If you prefer you can sign up for 6 months in advance and **SAVE £15.84** – that's still an impressive 20% off

FULL PRICE	PER-PAID SUBSCRIPTION PRICE	SAVINGS	MONTHS
£158.40	£118.80	25%	12
£79.20	£63.36	20%	6

- **FREE P&P** Your books will be delivered direct to your door every month for FREE

- **Plus** to say thank you, we will send you a **FREE L'Occitane gift set worth over £10**

  Gift set has a RRP of £10.50 and includes Verbena Shower Gel 75m and Soap 110g

What's more you will receive ALL of these additional benefits

- Be the FIRST to receive the most up-to-date titles
- FREE P&P
- Lots of free gifts and exciting special offers
- Monthly exclusive newsletter
- Special REWARDS programme
- No Obligation –
  You can cancel your subscription at any time by writing to us at Mills & Boon Book Club, PO Box 676, Richmond, TW9 1WU.

MILLS & BOON®

Sign up to save online at www.millsandboon.co.uk

P0KIT

SAVE OVER £39

WHEN YOU SUBSCRIBE

25% OFF

this, Ram—so don't you dare try to deny it. Not long in the planning?' she flung at him with a bark of triumph. 'These clothes are all in my size.' Her tiny hand swept dismissively down the exquisite suit she had selected to wear, with its priceless trimming of rare, cornflower-blue sapphires. 'How long would it take to put a collection like this together?' she demanded. 'You must have been planning this for ages.'

'You do look fabulous,' he said, refusing to be drawn. 'I'm guessing each piece will suit you equally well.'

'I have no idea about that,' she said. 'I wouldn't be wearing any of it if I had my own clothes to wear.'

'But, happily, you don't,' he said, and as he raised a brow he knew they were both thinking about her pirate queen get-up.

'This had better be the last surprise you spring on me, Ram.'

'Think twice before you say that,' he warned.

Ram was curbing a smile while she was scowling—at the thought that he was right. He had surprised her, and she wasn't used to gifts on this scale. She had no idea how to deal with presents from Ram any more than she had known how to react when he'd given her that dress all those years ago. And now her emotions were all over the place. Everything was happening so fast. Ram should have warned her they were sailing—but she was glad she was here. She felt so close to him—and yet she didn't know him at all, and all this made her feel vulnerable. 'You can't lavish gifts on me for no good reason.'

'I can't expect you to walk round in a towel either,' Ram pointed out. 'So, why don't we call it quits and go and have lunch?'

'What happened to breakfast?'

'You missed that while you were choosing what to wear.'

Unfolding his athletic frame, Ram came to stand in front of her. Taking hold of her hands, he drew her close. 'I just wanted you to have some treats. When we reach Ramprakesh things will be different.'

When had she heard something like this before? But she could only guess how different things would be for Ram, and had to force back tears when he tightened his grip on her hands.

'I've been running the country alongside my other business interests since my father's death, but it isn't enough, Mia. My people need me to stay with them. A distant playboy who issues directives from time to time is no use to them. They need my physical presence so I can put an end to all the corruption and make sure there's a strong government in place. That's why I've started building a house there. I don't want to live in some vast, echoing palace. I want to open all the palaces as institutes of culture. I want a reliable health service and education for all, and—'

'You have a vision,' Mia interrupted softly.

Ram thought about that for a moment. 'Yes, I do,' he said quietly. 'I want to slip into the country without any fuss and start work immediately. But until then… Well, why don't we make the most of our time together?'

Could she do that? Could she forget about tomorrow until they docked?

That didn't sound much like her, Mia concluded as she held Ram's gaze. But what lay ahead of Ram was so much bigger than anything she would have to face. 'You're right,' she said. 'What I should have said was thank you.'

'There's no need to thank me,' Ram assured her with a grin. 'Shall we eat now? Oh, and by the way—the Ramprakeshi clothes suit you.'

And with biting irony made them look like a couple, Mia realised, catching sight of their reflection in the mirror. Ram was wearing traditional clothes too, and his blue-black tunic with its Nehru collar not only toned with her outfit, but suited his exotic colouring perfectly. She couldn't help wondering what a man like Ram wanted with her when he could have anyone in the world. It wasn't long before more doubt demons crept in. 'This interior design work you mentioned—is that just something you made up to keep me sweet?'

'No, of course it isn't,' he said with surprise. 'You've seen the yacht—do I need to say more? Surely you don't think this is how I want to live?'

'And your house in Ramprakesh?'

'Will be very different too—maybe you can help me—'

'I'd love to,' she said, wondering if she wasn't taking on too much.

'You can do it, Mia,' Ram said as if he'd read her mind. 'I know you can.'

'You have a lot of confidence in me,' she said as they walked out onto the deck for lunch.

'Should I doubt you?' Ram demanded as he held her chair ready.

'No.'

'But?'

'No buts,' Mia said as she unfurled her napkin. In fact, no buts ever again. If Ram could do this—return to rebuild a country—surely she could handle a little redecoration. It was just a matter of scale—and, like everything else in life, confidence.

'It's all work in progress, Mia,' Ram assured her as he took his seat. 'This is as much a voyage of discovery for me as it is for you. Let's just say we're both embarking on a steep learning curve.'

She met his gaze and saw his vision of a better future for Ramprakesh. Whatever else Ram decided during this voyage she knew that from the moment he set foot in his homeland Ram would be an engine for change and the thought filled her with love and pride.

'Ramprakesh is a fabulous country, Mia. Wait until you see it.'

'I can't wait.' She gazed into his eyes.

'Would you like some bread?'

'Sorry?' It took her a moment, and then she saw that Ram's gaze was amused. He was telling her without words that this short, precious time was theirs and they shouldn't waste a second of it.

CHAPTER ELEVEN

THEY were hardly inside Mia's stateroom door before Ram was kissing her. This was everything she had ever wanted. Being with Ram had exceeded her dreams beyond anything she could have imagined and she couldn't think about the end of the voyage now—she refused to think about it. Ram's kisses were tender, passionate, cherishing, hot, and this was as close as two people could be—

And they were naked by the time they made it to the bed.

'Did you imagine one helping of Mia would be enough for me?' Ram demanded huskily as he turned her beneath him.

'I think we've entered the land of excess.'

'We're not even close yet,' he assured her, moving down the bed.

'Glutton,' she accused him mid-gasp.

'Are you complaining?'

'Certainly not.' Placing her hands on his shoulders, she put Ram to work again. 'I have no complaints—none whatsoever—except I can't hold on—'

'You're not supposed to hold on,' he said, taking her mid-scream of pleasure. 'And with every nautical mile we travel we're growing closer to that land of excess you mentioned...'

He wasn't joking, Mia realised as she moved with him, relishing each fabulous sensation as Ram transported her from a deeply satisfying conclusion to yet another hungry new beginning.

'Are you trying for a record here too?' she demanded some time later when she was still throbbing with sensation.

'You know how competitive I am,' he said, nuzzling her lips with his mouth.

'Don't ever change,' she murmured as a kiss became a caress, and the caress fired the hunger inside her.

'I have no intention of doing so,' Ram assured her as he took her again.

She didn't mean to spoil the mood, but the closer they became physically, the more she wanted to know about Ram. 'What?' he said, prompting her while they were briefly resting.

'There's something elusive about you.' Easing round in his arms, she stared into his face.

'Like all the stuff you won't tell me?' His gaze lingered on her eyepatch. 'School gave you the chance to try rally driving at an early age, and you used to be a good driver. What happened, Mia—when did you become reckless enough to bend a car round a tree?'

The recklessness had started on the night he left. But this was about Ram and she refused to be distracted. 'My injuries are out there for everyone to see. Yours are hidden,' she told him bluntly. 'And whatever you're keeping locked away from me can only have happened while I was in hospital undergoing surgery.'

'Very good, Miss Marple. Any more insights you'd care to share with me?'

'Don't make light of it, Ram. I just wish you'd share those secrets with me. I understand the responsibilities you're facing, and I know you can't take me with you into that world.'

Ram's answer to this was to stroke and kiss her brow. 'What did I tell you about making the most of this time?' he said, and, drawing her into his arms, he kissed her—

lightly, deeply, passionately… 'You worry too much about everything, Mia.'

'About you, maybe,' she admitted, finding it increasingly difficult to keep her feelings under wraps.

'I'm the last person you should be worrying about. I'm a mighty maharaja, remember?' Ram laughed as he mocked himself, a blinding flash of perfect teeth against his smooth dark skin. And then he kissed her again, and tickled her, until she had to beg him to stop, by which time she was crying with laughter.

'You don't need to offer me a job,' Mia murmured, lying warm and contented in Ram's arms after they had made love again. 'You're right about this being a wonderful adventure, but when I go home I'll almost certainly pick up my career—and that's thanks to you. You kick-started my brain, my ambition, my lust for life—'

'And for me, I hope?'

'Do you need to ask?' she said, sweeping a gaze down Ram's brazenly exposed body. He didn't even cover himself with a sheet. He just lay there, inviting attention—distracting her so she could hardly think beyond the next bout of pleasure. 'I don't need you to look out for me, Ram—nor must you feel you have to give me a job.'

'Who said anything about giving you a job?' Folding his arms behind his head, Ram stared at her. 'You'll have to compete for the various contracts along with everyone else. I can't be seen to favour anyone or that would mean a return to the old ways. I'm doing you no favours, Mia, other than putting you in the way of opportunity.'

'So…' She frowned.

'So?' Ram probed.

'Is that the only reason you brought me here?'

'I can't think of any other—can you?'

He had to move fast to dodge the pillow she threw at him. Mia wanted the type of reassurance he couldn't give. Their affair had been born out of their old friendship and curiosity, and then lust, but she was right to think it had turned into something more—and that was something he had to deal with before they landed in Ramprakesh, because then it would be all about duty. But right now... Winding inky curls of her hair around his finger as he caressed her face, he suggested she let her hair grow again. 'You have such beautiful hair.' And when she touched it, as if in surprise, he took hold of her hand to kiss each fingertip in turn.

'Is that supposed to show me that you care, Ram?'

She was still asking—and he was still on his guard. He would never lead her on. 'I care about you, Mia.' And that was as far as he could go. 'If my only interest in you was that you picked up your career I could have e-mailed my suggestions to you. Or, I could have asked one of my PAs to scour the trade papers and identify some promising opportunities.'

'I wasn't talking about work, Ram.'

He knew that.

'Is sex nothing more than recreation for you?'

'Surely friendship plays a part?' he suggested dryly.

'Friendship?' Mia laughed, a little sadly, he thought. 'I don't have many friends like you.'

'I'm pleased to hear it,' he said, tumbling her onto her back. He wanted her to laugh and smile and be happy. He wanted to make love to Mia until they'd both had their fill of each other, but deep down he wondered if that moment would ever come.

Ram knew just how to make her forget. Starting with her toes, he kissed his way up her ankles, her calves, her thighs, and all places north, until she was so hungry for him she didn't care what conditions he put on their relationship. But this time she wanted to be in control—this time she wanted Ram underneath her. And so she straddled him and took him deep, riding him with the same wild abandon she had always used to answer the stone wall she came up against with Ram.

If this was all there was...

She should have known Ram wouldn't remain submissive for long. He allowed her to enjoy him as long as he chose to and then he turned her beneath him. 'Enthusiasm and vigour are great,' he husked against her mouth, 'but neither one of them is any substitute for skill.'

And then he proved it, taking her to heaven and back with artful delay and intuitive strokes that allowed her to climb the mountain only to hover at its highest peak for the longest moment before plummeting down into the deepest pool of pleasure.

'How will I ever get enough of you?' she asked him when they lay quietly, recovering. She was already feeling the twinges of desire again. Incredibly, the more they made love, the more she wanted to make love with Ram. 'I'm addicted to you.'

She'd said too much. Confessions like that would only make things worse. An affair that could only last as long as the voyage couldn't be called addictive. At best, it could be great, or fabulous or exciting; but it could never be habit-forming, for that habit would have to be broken the moment they docked. 'What I meant to say,' Mia amended quickly, 'is, I'm addicted to your technique. Did you get all that out of a book?' She cocked her head to one side in the old, teasing way.

'All of it,' Ram confirmed straight-faced.

He laughed as he brought her into his arms. 'Don't you ever take life seriously, Mia?'

And now he could have cut out his tongue. Mia had to be the bravest person he knew, and all the bravado in the world couldn't hide the fact that she was still recovering. 'Do you ever take this thing off?' he demanded, lightly twanging the elastic holding her eyepatch in place. 'It's always so perfectly positioned.'

'Like your ego?'

He deserved that. 'You can take it off with me.'

'I know,' she said, making no attempt to do so.

'It makes no difference to me. You're the same person to me, Mia, with or without—'

'You think?' she said softly.

'I know,' he said, leaning on his elbows so he could look into her face.

'I'm bored of talking about me,' she said, and sitting up, she added, 'It's you I'm worried about.'

He shook his head wryly. 'Are you trying to change the subject, by any chance?'

She ignored him and proceeded to lecture him on the perils of fast cars and even faster living.

'When you're as old as I am,' he murmured, drawing her into his arms again, 'you'll understand.'

'I'll never be as old as you are, Ram Varindha. You'll always be older than me.'

'Can we save the philosophy and attend to more practical matters?' he suggested with a grin.

'If you mean, can we make love again...' She tried to act disapproving, but she wanted him again—*so* badly. It was as if they had never made love. And sometimes hunger—urges—needs, had to be *attended to*, as Ram put it so eloquently, before reasoned thought was possible.

'I want you—how's that for an answer?' Ram demanded as he thrust one hard-muscled thigh between her legs. 'And I can't wait while we debate it,' he added, pressing her knees back.

Any further conversation had to wait. Her words were lost as Ram began the delivery of pleasure in a way that demanded all her concentration. He was unequalled, she realised wildly as he gave her everything she needed in a firm and practised stroke. And he was everything she had ever wanted—

And it still wasn't enough, Mia realised when the shock waves had subsided, because rather than being the start of something wonderful and lasting between them this was leading towards the end. But it was incredible and she should be satisfied. It was far more pleasure than anyone could reasonably expect in a lifetime of loving, let alone during one passionate voyage on a billionaire's yacht.

As they lay together with their limbs comfortably entangled, Mia realised she was exhausted beyond the point of sleep. It was then Ram suggested they take a swim. 'Swim?' she managed groggily, her voice muffled by the pillow from which she didn't even possess sufficient strength to lift her head. 'You must be joking.'

'I thought we'd drop anchor by a beach and have a picnic.'

'Of course we will—you're serious?' she demanded when Ram sprang out of bed.

'Have you ever known me promise something I couldn't deliver?'

She watched him stride across the room, knowing there were some things Ram would never promise her, and she felt a stab of regret for all the things she couldn't make happen, however much she wanted to. And she hadn't forgotten her concerns for Ram. The seeds of curiosity had been sewn and she wouldn't rest until she knew everything that had happened to Ram over the years they'd been apart—and the shadows she'd seen flicker in his eyes told her she wasn't the only one to have suffered a trauma.

'I won't be long,' he called back to her from the door.

But with the hourglass running down, any parting from Ram was too long.

He showered and dressed and made the call to confirm that his arrival into Ramprakesh would be both discreet and low-key, the way he wanted it. Then he called the bridge and asked the captain to moor up at a beach they would shortly be passing. Moments later the giant vessel began to slow. 'Come on, lazy bones,' he said, coming back into the bedroom where Mia was still stretched out on the bed. He opened the doors leading out onto the balcony and threw them back. 'Get out of bed and we'll dive off the side and swim to the beach. I've asked the crew to bring us a picnic.'

'Don't you ever run out of energy?' she complained, hiding her face beneath the bedclothes.

'I'm sure you'll be the first to tell me if I do,' he said, crossing the room to whip her coverings away. Cupping her face, he kissed her.

'Are there any bikinis in the dressing room?' she said when he let her go. 'Of course there are,' she said, answering for him. 'You wouldn't forget a little thing like that, would you, Ram?'

'Little things I'm rather good at,' he told her with a grin.

'Big things too,' she murmured, her gaze slipping lower.

He shrugged and laughed. He had people to do everything for him—stock a boudoir, make a picnic, rule a country in his absence—but all of that was about to change. Why not make the most of every moment they had left? 'Are you getting out of bed under your own steam or do I have to—?'

'I'm getting up,' she screamed excitedly as he made to catch her.

'Five minutes,' he warned, 'and then I'm swimming to the island without you.'

'Don't even think it,' she warned him, disappearing behind the door.

She stood on the swaying bow rail what felt like miles above the shimmering sea, side by side with Ram, with her toes curled and her head back; waiting for his signal...

'Last one in is a—'

She had already dived in. She never waited for the word *chicken*. She had always had to go one better than the boys— that was half the problem of growing up with an older brother, Mia acknowledged as she struck out strongly for the shore. The water was cool against her heated skin and the currents were kind to them. Nevertheless, Ram was right beside her, keeping pace with her and guarding her, just as he always had. 'I can manage without you running gunshot,' she said the moment she felt firm sand beneath her feet.

'But you don't have to,' he pointed out.

'And I can walk—'

'But you prefer to be carried.'

She was right out of arguments. Night was falling swiftly, and overhead it looked as if ink were bleeding into the rolling grey clouds as Ram strode with her in his arms to where a shrubby green carpet of land met the beach.

'Do you ever take no for an answer?' she demanded as he lowered her to her feet.

'Only selectively,' he admitted frankly.

She laughed and swayed towards him. He dragged her close. They stared at each other and in that moment they were as close as two people could be. And then they began to laugh. This wasn't about sex. It was a celebration of a friendship that had survived against the odds. It was a celebration of everything they meant to each other, and it was proof that, whatever fate threw at them next, nothing could ever break the special bond between them.

But there were still far too many secrets, Mia thought as Ram let her go and stood back.

'So are you going to fill in all the gaps in your life for me?' she said. 'Or are you too important now?' Dragging him by the hand to where the crew were already laying out their picnic, she started to help out in spite of a chorus of protests. 'Or is it all one big secret?' she asked Ram as his staff made their way back to the small speedboats.

Ram chose to ignore her question. 'Choices,' he murmured, turning to the food. 'What's it to be, Mia? Truth, dare or chocolate…?'

'Normally, I'd find that quite an easy decision to make,' Mia confessed, tasting some of the delicious-looking finger food. 'But first there is something I want to know.'

'Truth, then,' Ram agreed.

'When you return to Ramprakesh, is it just a visit, or are you going back there to rule?'

'At present I'm nothing more than a figurehead, but I intend to change that.'

'You mean you want to get your hands dirty?' she said, reading him.

'That's one way of putting it. I certainly don't intend to stand on the sidelines any longer. My people need someone to work with them.'

'And in a country noted for its corruption, you're itching to get back there and put things right?'

'I am,' he confirmed.

'You're absolutely determined to stay and see this through.'

'Absolutely. Now, that's enough. It's your turn.'

Mia groaned, remembering this had started as a game—and there was so much more she wanted to know about Ram.

'And yours is a dare,' he said.

'Why aren't I surprised?' she said dryly.

'Take your eye patch off.'

Mia's growing confidence vanished in a puff of smoke. 'I won't,' she said. 'You can ask me anything else you like, but not that.'

Which was how she came to find herself belting out 'The Time Warp' to an audience of one on a beautiful Mediterranean beach.

CHAPTER TWELVE

AS THE days passed it was inevitable that Mia and Ram grew closer. And, yes, she was courting disaster, Mia thought as Ram's super-yacht began its stately progress through the Suez Canal. She was standing next to Ram, enjoying the greatest adventure of her life, knowing there could only be one outcome. Ram had his arm around her as if they belonged together as they watched the passing traffic, but that was an illusion. They were destined to be apart, everywhere but here on his yacht.

In some places the canal was as wide as a lake, and was called the Great Bitter Lake, Ram was explaining, while all Mia could think about was how quickly time was passing, and how she wished they had more time so she could enjoy this trip to the full. Ram looked so effortlessly sexy with his inky-black hair blowing around his wickedly handsome face. He had no idea, she thought as they waved to people in traditional houses lining the banks, how deeply she had fallen for him.

'Look at the fishermen,' he said. 'Wave to them, Mia.'

The men were rowing small boats with their nets bundled in the back, and in the distance she could see a super-tanker. There were pylons and industrial units, cheek by jowl with holiday flats and minarets. She had never seen such a mix of things and said as much to Ram.

'There's such a lot I want to show you, Mia.'

She hadn't meant her eyes to fill with tears, and turned her head away from him when he tried to blot them with his thumb. 'Do you mind if we go inside now, Ram?'

'No, of course not,' he said in a concerned voice.

She led the way—wishing they were in Ramprakesh—wishing this were over—wishing she could get on with the rest of her life.

Liar, Mia thought as Ram took hold of her in the shadows of the doorway. She wanted this to last for ever—and, like a child on its birthday, she refused to accept that the day had to end.

'I can understand that you're overwhelmed,' he said. 'I felt much the same way when I came here for the first time.'

Yes, that was it, she told herself, smiling up at him.

The days slipped by until they eventually sighted Ramprakesh. The country appeared through the haze of dawn like a magical, mountainous island, drawing them towards it. Ram left her to go and stand at the rail, while she had to forget a body singing from his touch and get on with her own preparations. She guessed that however quietly Ram planned to arrive there would be paparazzi on the dock. It was inevitable, and she didn't want to let him down.

She chose to wear a stylish, dark blue two-piece, another traditional *salwar-kameez*, and she teamed that with silky-soft leather sandals—not that anyone would notice, but even in the background she wanted to hold her head up high.

Being with Ram had ramped up her self-belief, Mia realised. After the accident she had gone from invalid to apathy and from there to wildly flailing about in search of a new identity. But now, and largely thanks to Ram, she had a purpose, which was to pick up the pieces of her career. And if she didn't win the contract to handle the interior design for him, it wouldn't be for want of trying.

Her heart lifted when she went up on deck and saw Ram staring intently at his homeland. For a moment she stood back just for the pleasure of watching him without disturbing him, but as always Ram sensed her close by.

'Mia.'

He sounded pleased to see her and reached for her hand. She went to stand beside him to watch the dusty land of green and gold fields drifting past.

They were cruising past a tea plantation, Ram explained, and the glistening rivers she could see in the distance fed those fields. Beyond the lush green hills there were purple snow-capped mountains. She thought it a dramatic landscape over which a striking man should rule.

People had started waving to them from the shore, and the excitement grew as they recognised the yacht and realised who was on board. Mia waved to a group of children lodged perilously in a tree and felt ridiculously thrilled when they waved back at her. How could she even think of taking Ram away from this—how could anyone?

Her emotions were all over the place, Mia realised as Ram shot her a look. The sense of impending loss was becoming unbearable, but she concentrated on the children, all the time hoping that she and Ram could at least go forward as friends.

'Are you crying with happiness?' he teased her when her tears refused to be driven back.

'I've got something in my eye,' she said impatiently.

'Can I help?'

'Too late,' she said, tipping her chin at a determined angle. Far too late. The damage was already done.

'Well, I have to say, you look absolutely lovely,' Ram commented as he swept an approving glance over her outfit.

'Right back at you,' she said, chirpiness cloaking her inner turmoil, though Ram did look fabulous in a black silk tunic and loose-fitting silk trousers that caressed his powerful body like a lover. 'There's only one thing that could improve your appearance,' she commented, 'and that's a smile.' She had never seen Ram looking so preoccupied.

'There's only one thing that could improve your appearance,' he said, staring pointedly at her eyepatch.

'And that's non-negotiable,' she said.

'Surely, you're not still worried about it?'

She knew her eyepatch was a source of constant irritation to Ram. He always referred to it as the enemy that kept some part of her hidden from him. 'I'm not worried about it at all,' she said. 'And as this is to be a quiet arrival and I shall stay in the background, it's hardly relevant.'

Ram said nothing. Perhaps her offer to stay out of the way was what he'd hoped for.

They didn't have much further to sail before the harbour itself came into view, and it was then Mia realised things hadn't gone to plan—at least, not to Ram's plan. She had never seen so many people waiting in one place before. The entire dock was a seething carpet of colour and life. Some people were clinging to lamp posts, while others balanced precariously on the rooftops. Every available square inch of space seemed to have been taken up by spectators, some of whom had even stacked themselves on each other's shoulders to get a better view. 'Wow!' Mia grabbed Ram's arm in her excitement. 'That's quite a reception!'

But all she could see on Ram's face was surprise and anger.

As the noise of the crowd reached them she tried again. 'News of your arrival has travelled fast—and that elephant you always wanted me to call for you? I think it's here.'

She was trying to lighten the situation, and in fairness the sheer fun and splendour of Ram's homecoming welcome was thrilling to see. Not so for Ram, apparently. He couldn't have worn a deeper frown—and suddenly Mia realised how that would look. Whoever had gone behind his back to arrange this could be dealt with later, but Ram should smile and show his appreciation for the warmth of his people's welcome. She pressed on with her own enthusiastic reaction to the festival atmosphere. 'I've seen elephants before, but never any as richly caparisoned as these.'

But this fell on deaf ears too. Meanwhile, ropes were being tossed ashore and officials were lining up. She could see a limousine with blacked-out windows waiting by the side of the dock and guessed the limousine had been Ram's preferred mode of transport before he knew anything about this reception. But he would have to adapt, and quickly, Mia realised, wondering who had designed this very different welcome home.

It was a shame Ram was so angry, but she couldn't help but be fascinated by all the new sights and sounds—the horns, the bells, the rapid pulse of chatter overlaid with chanting and shouting. The elephant parade was forming up now, and the mighty creatures were being fanned by the mahouts who would ride them. Judging by their elephant-sized jewels they had turned out to honour one man—though it was the people who were the jewels of Ram's country, and, forgetting her pledge to remain in the background, she began waving to the crowd. Lots of people waved back at her, but the focus of their interest was Ram.

Ram *was* Ramprakesh, Mia realised in that moment, and staring at him proudly she was glad for him and for his people. Just like the wonderfully vibrant country he was destined to govern, Ram was hot, spicy and exciting—and even a little bit terrifying, all rolled into one. 'Oh, Ram,' she exclaimed. 'To think all these people have come here to see you—

'Ram?' She pulled back to stare at him.

'This is not what you think.'

'What is it, then?' she demanded.

'A contrivance—a set-up—call it what you will.'

'A contrivance?' Mia exclaimed. 'You can't fake this, Ram. There isn't enough money in the world to pay all these people to come here.'

'No, but they have been misled.'

'By whom?'

'Just don't interfere in things you can't understand.'

Ram's rough tone shook Mia to her foundations. He had been her lover up to that moment, but now he was someone else—someone she didn't like too much. 'What have I said to upset you?' she demanded as he tried to brush past.

'Nothing. Now, please let me go. I can't keep the driver waiting.'

'The driver?' she shouted after him. 'Don't tell me you're going to climb into that limousine and sweep away when your people have gone to so much trouble to come to see you?'

'Well, I'm not riding a bloody elephant, even for you, Mia.'

She blocked his path. 'So drive away in your wretched limousine—I'll take the elephant.'

'And now you're being ridiculous.' He moved her aside and then was forced to shout after her. 'Mia! Come back here.'

She was halfway to the gangplank when she stopped, realising she was being impetuous. It was just that she had wanted everything to go well for Ram. But he was right. She couldn't just muscle her way into a procession intended for him.

Ram didn't want this fuss, so the person who had arranged it against his express wishes didn't know him if they thought Ram was so easy to manipulate. But if he took the limousine now as he had intended it would be a colossal PR blunder. Maybe the person who had arranged this did know Ram—and meant him to do the wrong thing. If someone didn't do something this glorious occasion could turn into a damp squib—a cheap celebrity event where the celebrity was rushed away behind blacked-out windows. And Ram was so much more than that.

He was greeting the first person in the line of officials when she arrived out of breath at his side. She wouldn't let him do anything he'd regret just because he was angry—

Much to the alarm of the security staff, Mia placed herself directly in front of Ram. He couldn't ignore her now, though he made it clear from his expression that she wasn't welcome, and he acted swiftly. Taking hold of her arm, he led her away into the shade.

'What do you think you're doing?' he said. 'Is this your idea of staying in the background?'

'I meant to stay in the background—but then you were so angry—and I don't understand why. I know you didn't want a fuss, but just think how long your people must have been waiting for you in this baking heat. All they want is to catch a glimpse of you, Ram.'

'Since when has the welfare of my people become your concern?'

'Human decency is everyone's concern,' she said firmly. 'Or it should be.'

'And now you're lecturing me.' Ram's eyes held such fire Mia wondered for a moment if he would simply turn his back on her and walk away. 'You don't understand,' he said. 'And I wish for once you'd just keep out of it.'

'Hard luck, Ram. You should know me better than that by now. I can't believe you'd give a welcoming committee of important people the benefit of your glittering presence and then sweep away in your fabulous limousine with its blacked-out windows so that the ordinary people of Ramprakesh don't even get the chance to see your face.'

'Are you so different?' Ram snarled at her, bringing his face frighteningly close. 'You hide behind your eyepatch like the coward you are, and then you have the audacity to criticise me.'

Mia took a step back. She could feel the blood draining from her cheeks as she stared at Ram, a man she'd thought she knew. But she didn't know him, Mia realised. This was a man who had been hurt to his soul, and who hid his wounds as carefully as she did. 'We'll do this together,' she said fiercely.

'What?' Ram demanded.

'I've always wanted to ride an elephant.' As she spoke she was already pulling the eyepatch over her head.

'There are photographers everywhere,' Ram said, shielding her.

'So what?' She stared at him defiantly, searching for any sign of revulsion in his gaze. Finding none, she felt her strength and determination grow. 'If the press ask any embarrassing questions, I'm a friend of the family,' she said, 'and you invited me to share this wonderful moment with you.'

'Mia,' Ram said, in a softer voice. 'They'll never believe that. They'll chase you to the ends of the earth, and your photograph will be flashed around the world.'

'So I'll get my fifteen minutes of fame,' she said carelessly, though her heart was thundering with alarm. 'I'm up for it if you are...I meant it when I said I wanted to help you, Ram. I'll help you in any way I can.'

'Then get out of here.'

'Not a chance.'

He didn't say anything for a while, and she really wasn't sure what would happen, but she'd played her cards and now she could only wait.

And then, miraculously, Ram frowned at her. 'Do you really want to ride an elephant?'

She had promised herself she would hold her feelings in, but that wasn't always possible. She was sure her face was jumping into a smile against her express wishes as she said casually, 'I thought I might give it a go.'

'And you also thought it would be more fun if we did it together?'

'Something like that...'

The last thing she had expected was that Ram would lift his hand and trace her scars; this was the same web of scars that gave her milky eye the appearance—or so the plastic surgeon had insisted—of a moonstone set in filigree.

She let one careless tear escape, but instead of wiping it away she tilted her chin at a defiant angle. She was determined weakness would not get the better of her this time, because this was Ram's moment, not hers. The surgeon had done a good job. Why not give her some credit? Mia reflected as she waited to see what Ram would do next.

'Forgive me, Mia,' he said softly. 'I shouldn't have allowed you to become caught up in this.'

But she wanted to be caught up...

'Come on,' he added briskly. 'We mustn't keep our taxis waiting.'

Elation roared inside her, but she behaved with absolute decorum while Ram went to make arrangements for a late passenger in the elephant parade.

This was the first time she'd gone without her eyepatch in public and she was shaking inside, but it didn't matter what she looked like, or what people thought of her, because this was about Ram fulfilling his destiny, and his happiness meant everything to her. At least he hadn't fainted with shock when he saw the full extent of her scars. He'd just given her a long, searching look that said Ram had seen everything he needed to. And now she must have that same strength for him. He was only one small step away from devoting himself to his people, and, yes, there would be enemies, and, yes, Ram still had some way to go, but he would be a great leader. She was sure of it.

A great stillness had fallen over the crowd and the only sound to be heard was muted chanting from the priests and the occasional jingle of bells. Ram had reached the end of the receiving line, and now he indicated that Mia must join him. She was still feeling elated and proud of Ram—right up to the moment when some elderly man dressed in finery bowed over her hand, murmuring, 'You have brought us a new queen, Majesty... How wonderful.'

She would have felt Ram's good mood shatter a football pitch away, but standing next to him was like experiencing a seismic tremor.

Ram—no! She told him with her eyes. He had to get through this without incident. There was something happening here she didn't understand, but, whatever it was, Ram's people were still waiting to greet him. 'I'm so very pleased to meet you,' she blurted out, muscling in in front of a seething Ram. 'I'm afraid I'm not your new queen,' she explained to everyone's astonishment. 'I'm just a friend of the family out here to offer some advice on interior design.' She had to admit, it sounded a bit lame, and she was glad when Ram steered her firmly away, but it also amused her that from that moment on he introduced her as his interior design consultant.

Finally they reached the gangplank where a uniformed chauffeur was saluting by the door of the official car. 'You're not going to change your mind, I hope?' she asked Ram fiercely under her breath. 'I promise I'll never speak to you again if you do.'

'Don't tempt me,' he growled back at her, but to her relief what he did next brought the biggest cheer from the crowd. Walking a few paces ahead of her, he raised both his arms in greeting.

To say Ram's people were ecstatic at this sign of his affection would be totally understating the case. Mia thought her eardrums might explode, and it was some time before the beating of drums and cymbal clashes could be heard above the cheering, but eventually the determined drummers formed up at the head of the procession of elephants.

There was a moment when a prolonged barrage of camera flashes made Mia feel for the eyepatch in her pocket, but she took her hand away; there could be no more dodging the issue for either her or Ram.

Ram's response to the adulation of the crowd was yet another incarnation of the man she loved. She had never seen him in this light before, standing with his hands clasped as if in prayer as he bowed to his people. It was a pledge of service she found both touching and inspirational. To have such a man on your side would be—

'Mia?' Ram's eyes searched for her as he turned, and he seemed relieved to see her. 'Your taxi's waiting...'

Well, she'd asked for this, Mia thought with amusement

and not a little trepidation as she followed Ram's gaze towards a huge, gentle-looking beast. The elephant was kneeling to allow her to climb into the lavishly decorated howdah on its back, and a mahout, or driver in turban and baggy trousers, stood ready to help her. Biting her lip, she laughed with nervous anticipation. There was just one more thing she had to check. 'You are coming too?' she confirmed with Ram.

'I believe that big old tusker is mine...'

Mia gasped. The biggest elephant she had ever seen, clothed in priceless armour of beaten gold, its crimson regalia flashing with the fire of rubies and diamonds, was a massive warrior beast almost as formidable as Ram. 'You're well suited,' she said when the mighty animal raised its noble head and bellowed as if in recognition of another king.

'Just go, will you?' Ram said, trying to look fierce, though his eyes were laughing. 'Just go ride your elephant and give me some peace.'

Mia relaxed into laughter, more relieved than she could say to see the fun back in Ram's eyes. His steely core had defeated whatever the old man had said or done to hurt him, for now Mia was sure that the wily courtier played some significant role in the politics of Ramprakesh. What? She couldn't know—but she was determined he wouldn't spoil Ram's day.

Once she was up in her swaying seat, Mia could see that the crowd extended for miles in every direction. Ramprakesh in carnival mood was a scene of incredible vibrancy, and she felt an immediate affinity both for the country and its people. The sun was blazing down from a flawless sapphire sky onto what had to be an unparalleled kaleidoscope of colour, scent and music. Drab beige was nowhere to be seen, and the air was zinging with the scent of food and incense and dust—and there were more flowers than she had expected in such a hot country—worn as brilliant orange garlands, or tossed like discs of sunlight into the air so that they landed around the giant feet of Ram's elephant.

The howdah was more comfortable than she had expected too, though she guessed this form of transport must have remained largely unchanged over the centuries. It was a unique privilege to share this experience with Ram. He was already wearing a garland of golden flowers around his neck, and the colour was a striking contrast against the sombre black of his silk robe. But it was when he pressed his hands together in the traditional greeting that she thought like a priceless black diamond Ram's darkly glittering glamour had finally found its true home.

'Are you comfortable?' he yelled as their howdahs drew level.

'Perfectly,' she mouthed back at him with a smile. Gold-fringed rugs protected their gentle giants' backs, while deeply padded cushions of crimson velvet invited relaxation. Each elephant wore a band of gold around its tusks and similar gold-trimmed headdresses from which spirals of gold wire and pearls cascaded down like giant-sized earrings, and a heavily ornamented brow band from which a jewelled medallion hung. She had no doubt the huge flashing jewels were real. No one had been left without a party outfit, she thought happily, wishing she could reach down to pat her elephant's papery side.

'Not bad for a lift from the docks?' Ram called out to her.

'Not bad at all,' she called back. She felt a great explosion of joy inside her as she watched Ram waving to the crowds. Seeing him so happy and relaxed with people who so obviously loved him meant everything to her. But there was still one question puzzling her. If she had been mistaken for the new queen, what had happened to the old queen?

There were many unanswered questions and only one certainty—Ramprakesh was a very different world, and one she would need a new rulebook to deal with.

CHAPTER THIRTEEN

THE parade was fabulous and exhausting as it lasted for hours.
It wound its way slowly uphill, along a broad, dusty avenue
lined every inch of the way with huge crowds. The sun was
setting by the time they reached the foot of some colossal
arched gates, and beyond these Mia could see a magical
walled city whose stone was rapidly turning pink in the fading
light. She thought it was like something lifted from the pages
of an exotic fairy tale.

It was a thrill when Ram insisted on helping her down from
her lofty carriage and yet another thrill when he escorted her
up the vast sweep of marble steps. 'You don't have to do this,
you know,' she murmured as uniformed guards with turbans
and sashes and scimitars hanging from their belts opened
the golden entrance doors for them, but Ram insisted, and,
wrapping his arm around her waist, he said, 'Do you think
I'd ignore you? What you did there back on the dock—'

'Was nothing,' Mia insisted.

'It was a little more than that,' Ram said with matching certainty. Cupping her chin, he raised Mia's face to his. 'You're
the bravest woman I know, Mia.'

'We both have our moments,' she told him lightly. 'Look
at you—riding an elephant. Who'd have thought?'

He laughed and let her go, but she hadn't forgotten Ram's
earlier reaction when he saw what a fuss had been made for
his arrival, and she filed it away for later consideration as he

led her on through the entrance portico towards the long line of staff waiting to greet them.

The Ramprakeshi were a gracious people, and they were a proud people, who didn't even try to hide the happiness they felt at seeing Ram come home. When Ram had greeted his staff, he showed her into a marble hall of such vast proportions there was room for a fountain complete with three full-sized marble warriors mounted on stallions that spouted streams of water from their yawning mouths.

'I had no idea,' Mia gasped.

'That I live so modestly?'

As Ram shot her a wry smile she could almost believe they'd left the shadows behind and that the idyll could continue for ever. 'I was thinking more of the extraordinary kind-heartedness and the welcome from your people. You must have missed them dreadfully.'

'Some are exceptional,' he agreed.

'And some are not?'

'A few of the courtiers and the professional hangers-on—'

'Ram, you don't need to explain to me.'

'But now you're here you should know,' he insisted, drawing her out of earshot.

'Are you referring to the old man who greeted you—the one who mentioned a new queen?'

Bullseye. Storm clouds gathered immediately in Ram's eyes.

'Not now,' he said.

'Perhaps I should know sooner rather than later so I don't put my foot in it. Can't you explain what he meant by your queen?'

The light in Ram's eyes had narrowed to a pinprick, but she was primed with insecurity and didn't know when to stop. 'I realise I'm not exactly fairy-princess material—'

'Stop that!' Ram snapped, shocking her into silence. 'This has nothing to do with how you look.'

Even if, right at that moment, she couldn't have felt more flawed?

'In fact,' Ram went on coldly, 'this has nothing to do with you at all.'

Opening the door, he gestured with a curt nod of his chin that she should go ahead of him. But she couldn't leave it here. 'Ram, please…I understand there are things in Ramprakesh I shouldn't interfere in.'

'And things you don't understand,' he emphasised as he started to walk off. 'You would be doing me a great favour, Mia, if you kept your opinions to yourself in future.'

'Ram, where are you going?' She glanced round, only to meet the concerned stares of the servants. What was she supposed to do now? The hall was the size of two football pitches and Ram had just taken off down one of the broad open-air avenues that bisected his enormous palace. 'Please come back.'

She only knew one way and that was forward. She ran after him, oblivious to the servants who were trying to direct her another way. 'Ram,' she called, angrily now.

He must have heard her, but he didn't even break stride.

Putting on a sprint, she caught up with him. 'You're right,' she said tensely. 'I don't understand. I thought I was a guest in your house, and at least in my house guests are escorted to their bedrooms by their host.'

'And what do you think the servants are waiting to do?' Ram demanded, staring somewhere over her head.

'Well, clearly you're right and I'm wrong,' Mia agreed. 'This is your house and your rules. Just leave me here and I'll make my own way to my room. Do you have a map I could use?'

'You're being ridiculous, Mia,' Ram told her impatiently. 'Just go back to the hall and they'll be waiting for you there.'

'They?' she snapped. 'Do *they* have names?'

He whirled around at that, all power and fury. 'It's you

who needs a reality check, Mia. This is not downtown Planet Space-Cadet, but a royal palace in an ancient land, where generations have worked side by side for millennia. Of course I know the names of my staff just as they know mine. What they couldn't be expected to know is that I'd be bringing someone like you along—'

'Someone like me?' she exclaimed.

'Someone with no respect for protocol at all.'

'Protocol? Or sheer bloody rudeness. Whatever happened to the courtesy of princes, Ram?'

'I think you've said enough. What exactly do you expect me to do, Mia?'

Explain what I should do—be considerate towards some-one feeling really out of place here? 'You could dredge up some civility, maybe? Considering—'

'Considering what?' he cut across her coldly. 'Considering I slept with you? Is that what you were going to say, Mia?'

'You didn't do much sleeping, as I remember—'

'I don't want to hear this—'

'I bet you don't. What's happened to you, Ram?' She clung onto his arm to stop him leaving. 'What happened on the dock to spoil everything? What did that man say that upset you so much? How can you change towards me so quickly? And how can all this leave you flat?' she demanded finally in exasperation. 'First the people on the dock and now the servants here who plainly adore you?'

'They're all being manipulated.'

'All of them? All those thousands of people who lined the route are being manipulated?'

'Yes, and by someone who doesn't want anything to change—someone who believes that showing off is more im-portant than dealing with the real issues. I'm talking about a man who lines his own pockets at the expense of the people, Mia—a man who lays on a bash like this to herald my arrival purely to seduce me into his way of thinking. Now do you understand?'

'I had no idea—'

'No, that's right, you don't,' Ram agreed, and this time she didn't try to stop him when he turned on his heel and walked away.

Mia wandered the ballroom-sized rooms of her suite, feeling out of place amidst such grandeur. She couldn't stop thinking about what Ram had said. She was lucky to be staying in what had to be one of the most beautiful palaces in the world, but all she really wanted was a cosy sitting room and a heart to heart with him. Ram's people had clearly enjoyed the parade, and on big occasions surely there was no harm in a festival cavalcade so long as the funds came from Ram's purse, rather than the public one. She hoped he wouldn't throw Ramprakash into deep austerity just because one evil man had used such occasions for his own nefarious reasons.

But Ram was right about turning this palace into a historical showpiece for everyone to enjoy, Mia mused as she traced the decoration on a wall with her fingertips. Richly enamelled in jewel-colours picked out in gold, the exquisite workmanship was a monument to the country's skilled craftsmen and this palace should be opened to the public so that people could see the riches they had inherited.

Thinking about Ram made her long for him, but she had no idea when she would see him again. Ram didn't have to explain himself to her, and his manner had been so volatile since arriving back in Ramprakesh she couldn't predict when he would turn up. She was only now discovering that physical intimacy didn't open the deepest portals in a person's mind, it simply drew a veil of pleasure over them. But there was no way she was going to wander about aimlessly for the rest of the day. Even if Ram was too busy to see her she still had work to do. She had done enough coasting since the accident and now she had a chance to put her life back in gear. She was itching to get started. She wasn't a tourist and she wasn't really a guest, and if Ram was serious about her submitting ideas for both his yacht and his new home, then the first thing she had to do was visit the site—which in turn meant having the right equipment.

She was smiling by the time she put down the phone. A requisition form would be delivered to her rooms immediately. Ramprakesh was nothing if not quaint.

Having completed the form, Mia folded it neatly and placed it on the golden platter that had been left in the room for that very purpose.

'You could have rung your order through—'

'Ram!' Mia's heart exploded in a frenzy of activity. 'What are you doing here?' She sounded angry—and yet she was so happy to see him it hurt.

Ram appeared as cool and sexy as always—as if they had never exchanged a cross word. Leaning back against the door with his arms folded, he said, 'I did knock, but you were too busy pacing to notice.'

'I thought you were too busy to see me,' she countered.

'I thought I'd better check you like your accommodation.'

'Finally,' she said.

'I had things to do when we arrived—people to speak to—'

'And a guest to settle in.'

'So you do like your accommodation,' he said, refusing to be thrown.

'You are joking? No one lives like this, Ram.'

'At least one person you know does,' he said dryly.

'But not for long.' Mia smiled.

'Yes, as you know, I have other plans. So, what's it to be, Mia?' Easing up, he came towards her, steadily, relentlessly, reminding her—and not for the first time—of some sleek, dark jungle cat. 'Am I in for storm-force tantrums or a fit of the doldrums?'

'Neither,' she said. 'But you do need a good shake.'

Unfortunately, that would mean getting closer than was strictly advisable right now.

'So what do you think of the palace?' he said.

'As a home for you? Overblown like the yacht—but it is a fabulous showpiece for the country.'

Ram had picked up the requisition sheet. 'You should have called me if you needed anything, Mia.'

'Why would I do that,' she said, still feeling needled, 'when you couldn't even spare the time to show me my room?'

'Please accept my apologies.'

But Ram was smiling—and he didn't sound one bit repentant. And now she was staring at his lips.

'Anything you want, Mia,' he murmured, coming to stand in front of her. 'You only have to ask.'

'Can I have my old friend back?'

Ram laughed, but she'd had enough of his erratic mood swings and was in no mood to stroke his ego. 'Why are you here?'

'Can't you guess?'

Excitement and shock coursed through her. Did he think she was really that available?

The answer to that was clearly yes, Mia realised, backing away from Ram as he steadily closed the distance between them. 'You can't—'

'I can't do what, Mia?'

'Whatever it is you have in mind.' Feeling a table behind her legs, she began to edge round it.

'I won't do anything you don't want me to,' Ram assured her as she put a sofa between them.

'Can't this wait until tomorrow, Ram?' Giving her time to firm up her resolve.

'Would you rather it did?' And now his wicked lips were tugging with amusement.

'Ram, you can't just—'

'Kiss you? Hold you?'

How did she come to be in his arms?

'You can always walk away,' Ram pointed out. 'No? You don't want to?'

'You know I don't,' she managed huskily.

'Careful what you say, Mia,' Ram warned, staring down into her eyes. 'Palaces have ears.'

And lips to whisper secrets, she thought, feeling her pulse rise in response to him while her distracted gaze sought out the exotic paintings on the walls. Erotic love appeared to be the overriding theme in Ramprakesh—as if she needed any encouragement.

'I think you've cast a spell on me,' Ram murmured as he pulled her deeper into his arms.

'I wish,' she said carelessly.

'What do you wish for, Mia?'

That Ram would take her now—here on one of the fabulous rugs beneath a ceiling composed of mirrors. But it would only be another sensory overload to help her forget that for ever with Ram was out of reach. 'No,' she murmured as he brushed her lips with his.

'No?' His gaze was both amused and compelling. 'Are you telling me you don't want this?'

Oh, so much...

Ram could be so tender. He made love to her as if they had all the time in the world. And she responded as she always did, like a glutton who could never get enough of him. He chose a conveniently placed bank of silken cushions rather than the rug on the floor, and now she was beneath him with her wrists held in a loose grip above her head as Ram slowly undressed her with his free hand.

Ram's hands were skilful and his kisses had completed the seduction. Her limbs felt as if they had flooded with molten honey and all she had to do now was wait to receive the pleasure that was coming. Ram knew everything there was to know about pleasure. He needed no prompting from the artwork on the walls, though it was an added fascination to see his reflection in the mirrors over their heads and to see her legs spread wide in invitation. Her breasts seemed fuller than usual as he teased her tight pink nipples with his tongue and with his teeth, and gradually her sensual movements on the silk supporting her became more urgent—the reflections in the mirror more blurred, and her fingers more demanding as she clutched and unclutched them, begging him to set her free.

'I rode an elephant for you,' he growled against her mouth, 'and now you have to pay.'

'I can't wait,' she assured him, arcing her body in the hunt for some desperately needed contact. 'Aren't you too warm like that?'

Ram laughed. He was only wearing a simple tunic in cream linen and some rather revealing linen pants.

'Let me undress you,' she begged him.

'And allow you to escape?'

'I'm not going anywhere.'

Ram's sexy mouth tugged in a grin. 'Somehow, I believe you…'

He was naked in moments, but then he turned her beneath him. 'Where were we?' he said.

'Somewhere around here,' Mia suggested, positioning herself on the cushions so she was sure she could see everything Ram would be doing to her in the mirrors overhead. Putting her arms over her head, she allowed him to capture her wrists again and then, drawing her knees back as far as she could, she slipped her legs over his shoulders. She was so confident of pleasure—so confident with him. And the sight of Ram's reflection—strong and powerful as he knelt between her legs—only added to her arousal. She had never seen him so engorged, so big, so firm, so hard, and when he allowed her just the tip, only to withdraw, she thought she would go mad for him.

'Enough?' he said, tracing a teasing pattern that never quite gave her what she wanted.

She couldn't speak—she could hardly breathe—

And then Ram sank deep inside her and began to move.

She climaxed immediately. She couldn't stop herself. The first she knew of it was when she heard herself moaning, shrieking, crying—and then she was clinging to him so fiercely she even missed the moment in the mirrors.

'Enough?' Ram suggested a second time, as she gradually subsided and sank back on the silken cushions.

'You don't play fair,' she murmured as he dropped kisses on her neck.

'Would you have me any other way?' Ram demanded, wholly unrepentant.

'Let me think about that.' She was already reaching for him again.

'How long do you need?'

'As long as you've got.'

CHAPTER FOURTEEN

MAKING love to Mia felt like coming home. His only regret was that Mia couldn't be part of his future in Ramprakesh. But he couldn't let her go, either—the details were sketchy...

The details hardly mattered as he sank deep into her welcoming warmth.

'Why are you so distracted?' she murmured, lacing her fingers through his hair as he kissed her.

You're everything to me, rang in his head. *For now*, were two words he would not contemplate, particularly when Mia's sighs of pleasure were drawing him back into their erotic world.

He made love to her as if it were the last time and she met him at every thrust, fixing her gaze on his, as if at some deep level she understood. She was beautiful and she wanted him, and when she lost control in a frenzy of gasps and screams he told her she meant everything to him, and he held her as if he would never let her go—as if some outside force were trying to wrench her from him and he was fighting it—but then he realised that the only demons he had to fight were within himself.

She had to learn the truth from a maid. That was what really hurt, Mia realised, sitting at her dressing table with her head in her hands. It was the following morning, and, in fairness to Ram, she hadn't given him much time to talk during the night.

But that was no consolation when she learned that Ram had left England to marry an arranged bride—a princess of equivalent standing—but his bride had died while Mia had been in the hospital, which was why she had remained completely out of the loop. Now she knew why Ram had been so angry at the dockside. The mention of a new queen made the tragic loss of life seem nothing more than an inconvenience. But why couldn't he have told her the truth? Why didn't he want to talk about it? Was Ram still in love with his lost bride? When the old man in the receiving line had suggested that Mia was the new queen, Ram's reaction had been one of anger...

She felt so hurt—so shut out. She had never presumed to see herself at Ram's side, but it was this silence on his part that hurt her. Intimacy was a confusing thing—it came with the expectations, at least where Mia was concerned, that it would bring you closer to each other. Yet now it seemed that she and Ram were further apart than they had ever been. The thought that Ram's tragic bride must have meant far more to him than she ever had really hurt. She might not see herself at Ram's side, but had never imagined it would be so difficult to think of anyone else taking up that place.

She was so confused. The only thing she could be sure about was that she couldn't bear to stare at her stunned-stupid self in the mirror any longer. It was time to get real. Ram had appetites—they both had—and that was all this was: an affair.

But he had made her feel so safe and special. He made her believe they were as close as two people could be. And suddenly she didn't feel so special. At least, not as special as Ram's lost bride must have been. He must have really loved her. And Mia could only ever come a poor second. She was someone Ram had used to blank his mind from all the pain he had endured—at best a bed-buddy to distract him. And it had taken a complete stranger to point this out to her—not in so many words, of course, but now she understood Ram's past and why there was always part of him she couldn't reach. She had always wanted to believe the fantasy when the truth was Ram would always mean more to her than she meant to him.

A rush of impatience hit her at succumbing to feeling sorry for herself—she had things to do. Springing up from her seat at the dressing table, she blundered about, swiping tears from her cheeks. Life wasn't all passion and romance—so she should get over it; get over Ram—or, go back to wearing an eyepatch and hiding from the world...

There was only one thing she could do, Mia concluded, snatching up her notes. She had to get over this fantasy affair and get down to work. She had to try to win the contract and prove she could survive without Ram. All this was her fault. She should have left him in the box marked Old Friends where he belonged and never have tried to shoehorn him into the very special box marked Soul Mate. Ram's soul was dark and complex and she'd had more than enough shadows in her life.

A brisk phone call from Ram's PA informed Mia that he would pick her up at eleven sharp. All the individuals tendering for contracts connected to his new home would be given the same guided tour, she was told.

She was ready on the dot, dressed in the work clothes that had been delivered to her room in accordance with her requests on the requisition sheet, and her mind was focused on the job in hand—pretty much. But there was an enormous elephant in the room—and not the kind she could ride. At some point she had to confront Ram with what the maid had told her. How could she rest until she had heard the truth from Ram's lips?

'Have you made any progress?' he demanded when he arrived, shooting a glance at the scatter of architects' drawings on the central table. He was dressed in work clothes too—blue jeans, heavy boots and a chequered shirt with the sleeves rolled back.

He looked…amazing, Mia thought—rugged, strong, and dangerously sexy. 'Some,' she said. Her heart was beating so violently it was hard to think. She wanted to scream at him, *Why didn't you tell me? Don't you care for me at all?*

But then he held out his hand and whispered, 'Come over here.'

She hated herself for doing just that—and hated him even more for not sensing the turmoil inside her.

'These sketches look good,' he said.

And now all she wanted to do was hide the upheaval inside her. Ram mustn't guess—not if she were to stand a chance of competing with all the other designers he had called in. How unprofessional would that be? *Mia can't contribute any ideas because she's in love with the boss…* 'They're only preliminary ideas,' she said more sharply than she had intended.

Ram shrugged as she ignored his outstretched hand. But how could she take it when touching him would only fill her head full of arranged brides instead of building sites? 'I need to see the site before I finalise anything.'

As Ram levelled a stare on her face she realised that he could play this game a lot better than she could—goodness knew what else he was hiding.

And did it matter when right now she had a job to do? 'I've been trying to work out how best to harvest natural light while protecting the occupants of the palace from frying in the sun.'

Ram's lips tugged in a grin. 'Air conditioning?'

'Of course.' Her skill was in interior design not heating engineering, but she still wasn't thinking straight after what the maid had told her.

'Are you ready to go?' Ram stared at her keenly.

She wanted to get everything out in the open right now—but how could she when everyone was waiting for them?

Ram *was* better at this game than she was, Mia concluded as he went up and down the coach exchanging pleasantries with everyone involved in the project. You would never guess he was hiding anything.

Maybe he just didn't see it that way. Maybe she was on the list of those to whom only limited information would be released.

'Okay?' he prompted, swinging into the seat beside her.

'Okay,' she confirmed. This was neither the time nor the place—and, in fact, why should Ram tell her anything about his private life? It was she who had blown their relationship up into something more than it was in her mind—though as she looked at his hands, so strong and capable, the thought of them caressing any other woman made her feel physically sick.

'You'll have to tell me what's on your mind sooner or later,' Ram said, catching her off guard.

'I was admiring this,' she lied, staring at the platinum wristband he never took off.

'And do you expect me to believe you?' he said. 'Are we keeping secrets from each other now, Mia?'

She was so taken aback she could only stare at him, and as he turned in his seat to speak to someone she felt another tidal wave of hurt wash over her. If Ram hadn't wanted to confide in her, why hadn't Tom said something?

Because her brother would never break a confidence. Because Tom would think she had enough to cope with recovering from the accident without filling her in on Ram's wedding plans...

'My new home will be built on the shores of that lake—'

'You never refer to it as a palace,' she said, pulling herself round in time to follow Ram's gaze.

'That's because I hope it will be a home,' he said. 'Mia?' he prompted as she stared out across the neatly groomed fields to the stretch of sparkling water. 'If there's something bothering you, why don't you just spit it out?'

'There's nothing bothering me.'

'What do I have to do to make you tell the truth?'

Ram's face was close enough for her lips to tingle in response, but this time she wasn't playing his game. 'Nothing,' she said, closing her eyes to shut him out—and failing completely. 'I was just admiring the scenery…and thinking how well the isolation suited you.'

'Ouch.'

She turned her face away from him.

The coachload of interested parties didn't leave the stunning site of Ram's new palace until dusk, but Ram's hand stayed her arm as Mia prepared to board the coach. 'Not yet, Mia—let them go.'

She waited while he said goodbye to some of the lovely people she had met who Mia guessed only wanted Ram to stay in Ramprakesh, and who believed that if he was happy with the finished project it would be another tent peg in the ground.

As the coach drove away he steered her towards a group of frowzy Banyan trees where a skeleton staff had been serving refreshments all day. They offered cooling towels now, and iced tea, but as they started to pack up Mia found herself wondering what Ram's staff had thought of his proposed marriage. Had they loved his arranged bride? Had Ram grieved for her? Was he grieving now? And then she found that, although her own feelings were mixed up, it was impossible to despise a lost princess; a girl who must have died so very young—

'Did I explain that my plans include a surprise for you?' Ram said, distracting her.

She looked at him blankly.

Taking the towel she now realised she was wringing between her hands, he handed it to an attendant.

'Are we walking somewhere?' she said as he turned away.

'I thought a ride—I need to clear my head.'

Ram needed to clear his head? But she couldn't help but be excited at the thought of riding with him again, and his tense expression softened into humour as if he felt the same way too. 'I'd better warn you our mounts are evenly matched,' he said.

'Oh, no...' Putting a hand to her chest, she pretended disappointment. Turning to look at the two horses cropping grass, she said, 'I'll take the grey mare.' The horse had a strong, compact body, and its ears pricked forward in eagerness as it picked up their interest and lifted its head to look at them.

Maybe this was just another memory she'd get to cherish—another pain in her heart when she recalled it. But why not? It was such a lovely evening. The colours were extraordinary—tangerine and crimson bleeding into a rapidly darkening sky—and whatever Ram had done, she still loved him; any conditions she might place on their future relationship could come later. 'Are you sure you want to race me?' She adopted the old, cocky attitude, hands on hips.

'I'll even give you a head start,' Ram offered.

She laughed. 'I don't need an advantage.'

She left him to mount the black gelding, and, springing into the saddle, she gave a whoop, and was off.

Ram's horse thundered alongside her. 'To the old fort,' he yelled.

She should have anticipated this, Mia reflected as she raced ahead of him. He was watching her back, though she suspected his challenge would be coming soon.

And she was right. When he was sure she was safe on the flat Ram overtook her with ease—waving to her nonchalantly as he powered past. 'You'll pay,' she shouted after him, but

her voice was lost in the wind. And then she laughed because
sometimes it was just nice to know you'd met your match.

Her legs had turned to jelly by the time Mia thundered under
the stone archway that led into the shade of the ancient fort.
'You could at least pretend you didn't get here so long before
me.'

Ram was leaning against a towering cinnamon-coloured
wall as if he'd been in that same spot all day. 'And now you'd
better catch me,' she warned him as she slid to the ground.
'I'm—'

'Out of practice?' he suggested, catching hold of her. 'Okay,
so now admit I had you well and truly beat.'

'I'll do no such thing. You had the better horse.'

'You had first pick.'

'Knowing how fragile the male psyche can be,' Mia retali-
ated, 'I decided to be kind to you.'

'Well, that'll be a first.'

She loved the sparring between them even as she felt all
the shadows hovering over them. And almost at once, as if
her thoughts had transferred to him, the air between them
changed, and was charged with all the things they hadn't said.
Wheeling away, she went to care for the horses. She needed
time to think—time to work out how to handle her feelings
for a man in a relationship that was going nowhere.

Undoing the girth, she lifted the saddle and then removed
the bridle and carefully set them aside. Ram did the same for
his horse and then they stood side by side as they watched
them gallop towards the nearest grazing. He reached for her,
but this time she stopped him. 'You asked me what was on
my mind earlier—I'm afraid you can't make it right with a
hug.'

'Then tell me why you're upset,' Ram insisted.

'When were you going to tell me about your arranged
marriage?'

He seemed stunned for a moment, and then he said, 'Who told you?'

'Does it matter? I found out.' She felt so shut out again—so hurt. 'I don't understand why you couldn't tell me. You trusted me enough to sleep with me—to bring me here as if we could just pick up where we left off. But we can't do that, can we, Ram? Because there will always be part of you that stays with her...'

She was sure Ram could have no idea how menacing his physical presence could be when he was angry, but she had no intention of backing down now.

CHAPTER FIFTEEN

MIA was facing Ram over a dusty courtyard in the middle of nowhere with a body that shimmered with the knowledge of his anger and a heart that was breaking apart. She had brought him to the same crossroads she was facing. She didn't want to be his convenient mistress, and yet she had always known he couldn't offer her anything long-term. He might turn his back on her now and walk away. He didn't answer to her—he didn't have to tell her anything. He could ride out of her life and she'd never see him again—

'Did Tom tell you?'

'No,' she said with feeling. 'My brother would never betray a confidence.'

'Who, then?' Ram demanded, bringing his face close enough to frighten most people out of their wits.

'A young girl,' she said, sticking her chin out, refusing to take a step back. 'You don't need to know any more than that—'

'Oh, don't I?'

'It wasn't her fault, Ram. No doubt everyone was talking about it—especially when I turned up out of the blue.'

Brushing past her, he walked towards the well to draw some water for the horses.

'What did you think I'd do?' Mia demanded, following hot on his heels. 'Did you think I'd laugh at you? Did you think

I'd be shocked to learn that you of all people would accept an arranged marriage?'

Ram was lowering the bucket into the well and kept his back turned to her. 'It was a long time ago, Mia.'

'Not that long ago,' she argued. 'You must have known all along—that's how these things work, isn't it? That's what you came back for—and somehow I never heard about it so your intended bride must have died while I was in hospital. But if you feel it's in the past isn't that all the more reason not to mind talking about it?'

'Why would I want to?' he said. Having collected the water, he unhooked the bucket and looked as though he was going to walk away and see to the horses without giving her another glance. But she wasn't so easily put off. 'You're not over this any more than I'm over what happened to me—and we never will be if we can't talk about it.'

'Spare me the amateur psychology,' he said, walking on.

As she watched him coolly pour the water into an old horse trough a volcano erupted inside her. 'So what were you thinking when you slept with me, Ram—when we had sex? Were you thinking about her?'

He moved so fast she lurched back and almost overbalanced. 'Don't,' he warned with an angry gesture. 'Just leave it, Mia.'

But by this time she was shaking with passion. 'Oh, I see,' she spat back. 'Your intended bride was too pure to speak of in the same breath as me. I'm more your—'

'I warned you—' he said, taking hold of her.

'Let go of me,' she raged back.

Lifting his hands, Ram turned his back on her with a snarl of anger.

'I thought you trusted me, Ram. I thought we were friends, but you used me.'

'No more than you used me,' he said, turning to confront her. 'There are just some things I never talk about—to anyone, Mia. And that includes you.'

'But not Tom,' she said, thoroughly fired up by now. 'And I don't imagine your arranged bride was shut out either—'

'Leila—' Ram interjected. 'Her name was Leila.'

The tone of his voice was a spear in her heart. She had never heard Ram speak with such reverence, or such regret. But she had to punish herself some more…for doubting him; for hating a poor dead girl. 'So who was she, this Leila?'

'She wasn't you,' Ram said flatly.

His face was totally shut off to her, and she had to wonder how many spears one heart could survive. She had lost this battle. She couldn't fight a dead girl who still held a place in Ram's heart. But she did want to hear about her—she had to hear about her or she would never rest. 'Go on,' she said.

'Leila was part of my early life—we grew up as children together in the same royal nursery, cared for by staff.'

'So you formed a unit?' Mia guessed.

'A tight unit,' Ram confirmed.

'So Leila was very special to you?'

'She still is.'

She watched as Ram returned to the well for more water, wondering what her place was in all this. 'And that's it?' she said.

'What more do you want to know?'

Snatching the bucket from his hand, she tossed it to the ground. 'I'd like to know where I figure in all this, Ram—or don't I?'

'I knew you'd overreact if I told you.'

'So you weren't going to tell me?' Mia demanded incredulously. 'Let me tell you what I think, Ram. I can't believe you, of all people, would agree to an arranged marriage unless you wanted it.'

'I've already explained that I was younger and keen to conform.'

'So, what am I to you, Ram—part of your rebellion? Or am I just any woman in your bed?'

He grabbed hold of her. 'You're none of those things—
you're special to me in a very different way.'

'Should I be pleased about that?' She could feel his power
and the heat of his body only a whisper away from her, but
this time she clung to her pride. 'I guess I'm everything
Leila wasn't,' she exploded in a frenzy of failing confidence.
'Difficult, demanding, and ugly to boot—'

'No!' Ram raged. 'Don't you ever say that. You have to
understand, I was a different person then, and if Leila and I
had married it would have been a disaster. She was like a sister
to me, Mia. It would have been...' he grimaced '...wrong.'

The thought that Ram might not have wanted to marry
Leila was a bombshell she hadn't expected. She remained
silent as he pulled his shirt over his head, unhooked the bucket
from the rope and poured the icy water slowly over his gleaming torso, groaning with pleasure as he shook his hair out of
his eyes.

'And that's it?' she pressed.

Hooking the bucket up, Ram lowered it again. 'That's it. A
good friend died. But marriage?' He shook his head. 'Back
then I still thought I had to go along with tradition.'

'And now?'

'Now I make my own rules.' He let her digest that for a
few moments, and then asked if she was reassured.

More than she had expected to be. 'I'm sorry,' she admitted
in a subdued voice. 'It seems I might have jumped to conclusions and been a little hasty this time.'

'This time?' Ram murmured beneath his breath. 'Would
you like to freshen up?'

She should have seen it coming. She should have seen a
lot of things coming, Mia realised, shrieking at the extremes
of temperature as Ram tossed a bucket of freezing water over
her overheated body. 'I hate you!' she shouted as Ram threw
back his head and roared with laughter.

'If you could see your face.'

'I really hate you,' she assured him when he dragged her close.

'Just remind me—what is it they say about hate, again?'

'You can forget that! On this occasion hate absolutely means—'

His lips crashed down on hers, silencing her. She fought him, but not so hard he'd let her go.

'Next time I'll be sure to ask permission,' Ram assured her as she swiped her swollen lips on the back of her hand.

'That's what you think—but there won't be a next time.'

'Until the next time?'

He yanked her close and silenced her a second time; this time with a kiss that stole her breath away.

'You don't make it easy to understand you, Mia.'

'Says the sphinx—and anyway, easy's boring,' she told him, scowling as she slapped water off her drenched clothes.

'Do you think I don't know that by now?' Ram murmured as he brushed sodden straggles of hair from her eyes.

She wasn't quite over it yet. 'Friends owe each other the truth, Ram.'

'Friends?' Angling his chin, he raised a brow as he stared down at her.

'If we were true friends you could tell me things you couldn't tell anyone else…' Her voice tailed away. Suddenly she felt very vulnerable indeed, but Ram just smiled his easy smile. 'Let's have a picnic,' he said, 'and I promise to tell you everything.'

He had brought a rug and some basic supplies on the back of his horse, and when he'd unbuckled the saddlebags and revealed the treats they laid everything out on the relative comfort of a mossy bank just outside the old stone walls. Uncorking the water bottle, he handed it to her, and Mia listened quietly as Ram told her about his childhood friend: a little girl called Leila who was basically the only family he'd known in those lonely days—a little girl he'd played ball with, and who had grown up to become his prospective bride, only to die tragically shortly before their wedding.

'How can you be so sure it would have been such a disaster to marry Leila?'

'The same way I'll know when a girl is right…'

His eyes were glinting with humour and she didn't want another row. 'So, tell me about her.'

'I hadn't seen Leila since she was little, and in all the years we were betrothed I only met her twice—'

'Twice?' Mia interrupted with surprise.

'The arranged marriage system here in Ramprakesh may seem odd to you, because you come from a very different culture, but Leila's family and mine were always close.'

'And you trusted your parents to sort everything out?'

'That's just the way it was,' Ram explained.

'And what did Leila think?'

'That she was the luckiest girl in the world, naturally—'

Ram choked as she gave him a whack. 'And now?' she said, having allowed some quiet time to pass. 'How do you feel about Leila now?'

'I feel sad,' Ram admitted, 'because she died so very young.'

She could only feel sorry for Ram's loss, and for Leila, a girl who had been groomed to be a queen without having any of the freedom and opportunities Mia had enjoyed.

And had been on the point of throwing away, Mia remembered, thinking about her languishing interior design career. She knew then in that moment that she could leave Ramprakesh with or without the contract for Ram's projects and still pick up her life—

Without Ram…

There wasn't room for another spear, she told her wounded heart firmly. 'What about now?' She dropped the question in casually. 'How would you feel about an arranged marriage now?'

'It could never happen. I'm back in Ramprakesh to establish

new traditions, not to blindly follow those I don't agree with.'

'A rule-breaker?'

'I'm an individual, Mia. I make my own decisions.'

There was one thing she still didn't understand. 'Why did Leila's death leave you feeling so bitter? I agree it was a terrible tragedy, but it was hardly your fault.'

'It was an illness, swift and brutal. The man you met at the dockside was Leila's father. He represents the council as it stands until I introduce a democratically elected government. When Leila died he couldn't even wait a decent interval before suggesting a list of new prospects.'

'Maybe he just wanted to keep you here?'

'I'm prepared to believe that of some people, but not him. He was only interested in promoting those girls whose families he could manipulate.'

'And continue on with a lifetime of corruption.'

'Now you understand,' Ram murmured. Tracing the line of Mia's cheekbone with his fingertip, he added softly, 'You always want to think the best of people.'

'Except you,' she said wryly. 'So that's why you left Ramprakesh—and why, when Leila's father met me at the dock, he thought I was your new queen. Perhaps he was already trying to work out how he would manipulate me.'

That made Ram laugh. 'He would discover he had bitten off more than he could chew if he took you on.'

Mia shrugged and smiled, but then her face filled with concern again. 'Everyone isn't like Leila's father, Ram. You've seen the people and how they adore you. Don't turn your back on them—or deny them the occasional festival just because that man used occasions like that to dazzle people so they didn't look any deeper.'

'Wise Mia.'

'I think we've both grown up.' She lay back on the mossy bank. At least Ram's heart wasn't taken, so that was good.

Where there was life, there was hope—right? She closed her eyes and felt him stretch out his legs alongside her.

'Shall I fix a marriage for you while you're here?' he murmured.

She snapped alert, only to find Ram's sexy gaze looking down at her. She sat up properly. 'I'm not some bargaining counter you can dangle under the council's nose to distract them while you reorganise the country. I'll marry who I want to marry…' There was only one man she could ever marry—and as that was out of the question. 'Or, maybe I'll never marry.'

Ram whistled softly under his breath. 'Do I have your permission to broadcast that? Only I think men everywhere deserve to know they're safe.'

'Just no more talk of arranged marriages.'

'Unless I do the arranging.'

'Keep out of it, Ram,' Mia murmured, suddenly feeling unutterably weary. Brushing a leaf from her face, she fell silent and a kind of peace fell over their casual picnic with its far from casual discussion, and though they were dozing side by side in the warm night air, Mia felt as far from Ram's heart as she ever had.

CHAPTER SIXTEEN

WHEN they woke the moon was like a lantern high in the sky shining down on them, and Ram reminded Mia that the lake was only minutes away on horseback.

'Shall we ride there bareback?' she said. 'Give them chance to cool their legs?'

'Why not?'

She couldn't think of a single reason.

The idea to take the horses for a refreshing swim soon developed into one of their adventures. First they had to race each other at full tilt beneath a canopy of stars, and when they finally reached the shore of the lake Mia was forced to admit defeat, but only by a few yards this time. But if they were friends, she reasoned, there was always a chance she could beat him next time.

'Enjoying yourself?' Ram asked her as their mounts moved deeper into the refreshing water.

'So much,' Mia exclaimed as her game little mare lunged forward and began to swim. Throwing her head back, she dragged deeply on the fresh night air. Surely it wasn't possible to feel closer to another human being than this—

Or to be more certain that the intimacy of tonight must end and she was again guilty of longing for things she couldn't have.

So, make the most of it, she told herself silently—this night was more than most people experienced in a lifetime, and if it only lasted five minutes they would be the best five minutes of her life.

They allowed the horses to swim for as long as they wanted to—neither Ram nor Mia was in any hurry to bring the night time idyll time to an end. It was as if they both sensed life catching up with them, and knew it could never be as straight-forward again.

Ram dismounted first and reached for her. 'Are you going to get down?' he said when she hesitated.

When she did it would be the end.

She could dodge reality, but she couldn't avoid it, Mia concluded as she slid into Ram's waiting arms.

'You're cold,' he said, embracing her. 'I'll build a fire and make you warm.'

All he had to do was hold her.

'Take your wet clothes off,' he said.

Ram was still half naked and cool from the water, while Mia's work jeans and shirt felt like a very heavy second skin. 'Ram, we shouldn't—'

'It's already done,' he said, tossing her shirt aside. 'You'll never get warm if you stay in those wet clothes.'

'I mean, you can't keep on doing this and expect me to feel nothing.'

'That's not true.' His lips tugged in a grin. 'I expect you to feel lots.'

And now she was laughing and aching for his touch, and common sense was out of the window. 'You can't,' she insisted, putting up the weakest protest of all when Ram's fingers found the fastening on her jeans.

'Of course I can,' he argued. 'In fact, I'm very good at it.'

'Egotist.'

'Contrary woman.'

'Smart ass.'

'Obstinate—awkward—difficult—' As Ram was punctu-ating each of these accusations with a kiss, it was very hard to argue with him. 'It's not that I don't want to,' she admitted, shifting position to make things easier for him. 'It's just that—'

'Like I said, you're contrary,' Ram growled. 'But I think you want me—am I right? And I know I want you.'

'Then, why ask a question you already know the answer to?' she said while she was working feverishly on his belt.

'Is there something wrong with a healthy appetite?'

'Nothing at all,' Mia admitted, shivering with arousal as she felt Ram's erection, huge and hard, pressing insistently against her.

And if this was all there was—

It would never be enough.

He kissed away Mia's tension, soothing her down and firing her up just for the sheer pleasure of seeing her so hungry for sex. There were no complications—nothing, except appetite and a long night of love ahead of them. In the morning he had to return to the city and his duties in Ramprakesh, but for now…

Governing Ramprakesh was a fact that had seemed a fiction for far too long—until he'd returned with Mia, he now realised. Seeing everything through her eyes had changed him. He had always known there was a lot to be done, but now he knew he could never leave his people to those who would abuse them.

'Kiss me,' Mia insisted fiercely, sensing his distraction.

He needed no encouragement. It was all too easy to lose himself in making love to Mia and allow all his other concerns to drift away. She was always hungry for him as he was for her, and he doubted that they could ever get enough of each other. He'd never met anyone like her, so cool, contemporary and strong—and unpredictable, he registered with pleasure as she muscled him to the ground. He loved everything about Mia. He loved her smooth, damp body, still chilled from the icy lake water, and the quick way she responded to him—

'Stop thinking,' she insisted, momentarily pinning him beneath her. 'You have to stop life dragging you this way and that.'

'Only you do that,' he argued, swinging her round so that now he was on top.

'You've always had too much, Ram—that's your trouble—'

'Not yet I don't,' he argued, stripping off the rest of her clothes.

But Mia was right. Where they went from here was up to him. The playboy years were behind him and it was time to live a different life. And Mia was right about him having too much. He could have anything he wanted and sometimes even that wasn't enough for him.

Ram had never made love to her like this before, Mia registered as he eased inside her. He was so gentle and loving... so caring—

Was this the long goodbye?

She had to tell herself not to be so melodramatic, or she would cry— Too late.

'I hope you're crying with pleasure,' Ram growled as he dropped kisses on her cheeks and on her lips and on her nose.

'You weren't supposed to see.'

'Well, I did see. Wasn't it you who said we shouldn't have secrets from each other?'

'I don't have any secrets, do you?'

'I have one or two up my sleeve.'

'How am I supposed to think straight?' Mia demanded breathlessly as Ram proved that was the case.

'You're not supposed to be thinking at all.'

'And as for keeping secrets up your sleeve,' she managed between noisy gulps of air.

'Okay, the place I keep them wasn't all that accurate.'

'You don't say,' she managed before sensation became her world.

Was she brave enough to pretend that unbelievable sex with Ram was enough for her, and that she didn't need for ever? Or would longing for Ram become her melancholy theme? She couldn't think about it now, Mia realised as Ram upped the tempo and she urged him on in a frenzy of desire.

This was enough. It had to be.

It was almost lunchtime the next day when Mia woke with a body aching pleasurably from Ram's exhaustive attentions. A limousine had collected them from the fort, transporting them back to reality in the early hours of the morning, while grooms took their horses back in a transporter. That was how things were done here; everything was so easy—easy for Ram, that was. But even as she stretched and kicked her brain into gear Mia refused to dwell on things that couldn't be and made sure she concentrated on things she could do something about—like landing the interior design job, for instance.

She took a shower and then told herself she would not look for Ram crossing the courtyard—nor would she listen for his voice as he strolled with his council in the garden beneath her room…

Like now? Standing outside on her balcony, peering over it with her ears pricked?

Okay, so she'd heard his voice in the distance. And now she could see he was walking with Leila's father. Both men's heads were close—though Ram seemed to be doing most of the talking.

Mia's heart sank. The photo on the front of that day's *Ramprakesh Times* had shown Ram standing with Leila's father, and a young girl.

Why did she always have to learn about Ram's plans from a newspaper? She backed into the bedroom before she could be seen. And why did Ram have to look so sexy, even when she could cheerfully batter him over the head with the collection of news articles she was steadily building up? How was any woman supposed to think straight in her position, let alone contemplate sharing so much man?

She couldn't. And that was that.

She had just completed her preliminary chat with the committee Ram had set up to decide who should get the commission to redecorate his yacht and design the interior décor of his new home. Had it gone well? Mia thought it had. She had kept her mind firmly fixed on business, and everyone seemed to like her ideas.

'Mia.'

Ram had followed her out of the room.

'You did well in there—better than even I imagined.'

'You're too kind,' she said dryly.

'You were the final element I've been looking for, and now everyone is talking about the benefits of an eco-home and gifting this palace to the people for education and tourism, as well as paring down the court to concentrate on providing more tangible benefits for the country—with the occasional festival thrown in, of course,' he added, his lips curving with amusement. 'In short—they liked your style.'

And she liked his. Concentrating on business was never going to be easy, Mia realised, thinking how well the traditional clothes suited him. The flowing black silk decorated with the finest gold embroidery and precious jewels hinted at the muscular form beneath.

'Everyone was impressed that you had researched the practical benefits of your design work as well as the aesthetics.'

'I did get a bit carried away,' Mia admitted.

'You were impassioned and yet coolly precise.'

'Why, thank you, sir.' She offered him a mock curtsey. 'Just doing my job.'

'Accept a compliment for once, will you?' Ram turned away briefly to acknowledge some servants as they bowed to him.

'Yes, Your Majesty,' Mia said cheekily, thinking how

magnificent Ram looked in his royal regalia and wondering if he was naked beneath the robe. Needless to say, he felt the vibes.

'Having exceeded my expectations as well as those of the committee, I can only conclude I'm giving you too much time alone.'

'Ram,' she warned him softly as more servants hurried past.

'There is one condition I must make before you go through to the next stage.'

'Which is?' Had she overestimated her success in the committee room? Mia wondered as Ram backed her into a side room.

'Can't you guess?'

'Are you mad?' She shot a glance at the door. 'Ram, you can't do this.'

'If I didn't know you better I'd think you were serious.'

'I am serious.' She pressed her hands against his chest, surprising herself with her iron resolve. This could go on for ever—if she allowed it to. She couldn't envisage a time when she wouldn't want Ram, physically, mentally—in every way there was. But now he had given her a chance to get her life back on track she should take it. 'I want more than this, Ram.'

'More?' he demanded, trying to keep a straight face.

'More of you...' Mia's voice barely made it above a whisper.

'I'm not sure I have more to give, Mia—you've got it all.'

'I'll always want you, so you know you can always have me...but when you tire of me, Ram—'

'When I tire of you?' he demanded, frowning.

'People do tire of each other.'

'Then they're not me,' he said softly. 'And they're not you.'

Shaking her head, Mia turned away. She didn't trust herself to speak, but she had to. 'I want a chance at this job, Ram. I ask nothing more of you than that. I think perhaps we should stop sleeping together.'

He didn't press her. He stood by his vow never to promise Mia anything he couldn't deliver, and right now his determination to disassemble the monarchic system in Ramprakesh and replace it with a democratically elected government was taking up all his time. He wanted to work for his country—and if the people wanted him as their leader, so be it, but standing at his side if that happened was a lot to ask of Mia. He'd had a lifetime to prepare for it. She hadn't.

He shouldn't have let this get so deep, he realised as he stared into Mia's wounded eyes, but he couldn't help himself—when Mia came back into his life she became his life. He also had to admit that a platonic relationship between them was something he had never considered, but if that was what Mia needed to happen...

'This isn't a game to me, Ram,' she said, calling him back to the present. 'It's the rest of my life I have to consider.'

'Well, on the professional front you should have no worries. You were outstanding today—and with very little time to prepare.'

'But can I do it without you?'

'Of course you can,' he exclaimed. 'But I guess that's something you can only find out for yourself—' And then a terrible suspicion swept over him. 'You're not thinking of leaving, are you?' The thought that she might return home and tender for the project from there had hit him like a truck.

She refused to look at him and, walking to the door, stood with her hand on the handle. 'I don't know—I need time, Ram—'

'There is no time,' he said impatiently. 'This is the real world, Mia. Not some fantasy land of your own creation—'

Raising her chin, Mia gave Ram a long, assessing look. He'd changed, and practically overnight. He was still as cool as ever—still as sexy, but young, hot and royal had transformed into a man with his hands firmly wrapped around the reins of power, and, while that was an added aphrodisiac, it was also a warning that if she didn't get her act together fast, he would leave her behind. 'I'll see you later,' she said, and before he could answer she left the room.

CHAPTER SEVENTEEN

HE SHOULD have known you couldn't leave a country without a leader and expect to return and find everything in perfect order, but at least his plans were in place now. Leaning over the carved marble balcony outside his apartment in the palace, Ram took a moment to stare across the moonlit plain. There must be no doubt in anyone's mind that he was back. Those courtiers who were corrupt or who thought they could manipulate him would soon learn that he was not the impressionable youth who had left Ramprakesh all those years ago. There were things he would set in motion right away, and others that could wait. And Mia was top of that list. She was strong and she would cope—she just didn't know it yet. He was confident, both in her abilities and in her resilience and strength. Sometimes he thought he knew Mia better than she knew herself. She had seized the challenge he'd set her and had exceeded his every expectation. Yes. Mia was more than ready to take her first step out of the nest. She had to try those wings of hers and discover that they hadn't been clipped by the accident, and that in fact her trials had only made her stronger.

By 3:00 a.m. she had a skeleton plan along with a spreadsheet of costings to put in front of a bank. She was going into business as an interior designer; she wasn't playing at it. Tom had already agreed to put up some of the surety, but had warned Mia that she would need more money to pay her suppliers.

And she'd get more money. Somehow...

Fretting, she nibbled her nails. Ramprakesh was almost six hours ahead of London, which didn't give her enough time to speak to the bank before her second meeting with Ram's council. There was nothing she could do about it and so she had made every safeguard she could, breaking the assignment into manageable stages so that the financial risk was reasonable.

With the first stage of her plan in place she called down to the kitchen for some food. She could get used to this sort of life, Mia reflected wryly, though Ram had made it clear that he had very different ideas. When it came to the design of his new home he would be using the kitchen, he had told her, and so it had better function well. Cooking was Mia's passion too, and she couldn't help imagining them jostling each other in the kitchen. She intended to give that area her special attention—

Like the bedroom?

Her smile faded as her glance darted to the door. For all her protestations of wanting a chaste relationship with Ram from now on, she had left the door unlocked. Wishful thinking? She was beginning to think so. Ram had moved up a gear and out of her life—

But at least she was on the verge of a new life too—

A life without Ram...

It was the early hours of another morning when she pulled the bedclothes tight around her shoulders, but she felt still stiff and cold and small. There was so much on her mind—Ram, mostly. She had to forget about him and see this stay in his country as purely an opportunity to widen her horizons. If she could do that she would have a future when she left here—

And if she couldn't?

She could waste her whole life pining for him.

She had to learn how to leave the bad boys alone and choose men who were more like comfy slippers—at which point she mumbled something very rude about maharajas.

'Talking in your sleep, Mia?'

She shot up like a loaded spring.

'That's a very bad sign.'

'Ram!'

She grabbed a sheet and covered herself. 'Where are you?' She could hear him, but she couldn't see him clearly in the shadows. She held her breath, but Ram moved like a panther in the dark, crossing the wide expanse of floor on silent feet. 'You can't just—'

She gasped as he threw himself down on the bed—apparently, he could. 'Ram, I thought we agreed—'

He turned his head to stare at her. 'You left the door open, and so I thought—'

'If the door was unlocked it was a mistake.'

Too vehement. He would know at once it was a lie. She dragged the sheets around her even more securely as she asked suspiciously. 'Have you been in the gym?'

'You noticed...'

It was hard not to notice. Moonlight framed him, and beneath his top she could see all his muscles were massively pumped and deliciously delineated. 'Ram, it must be almost dawn.'

'And you're still awake,' he observed with a grin, 'so it seems we keep the same crazy hours.'

'But you can't just come here and expect me to—'

'Expect you to what?' he interrupted, his wicked smile flashing in the darkness.

'To...' She was stuck. 'To entertain you?' she said finally, feeling her resolve melting like snow before the sun. How was anyone supposed to resist Ram in sports shorts and a tight-fitting top with muscles everywhere? Even his feet were sexy—*especially when they were entwined with hers?*

'Did I say anything about you entertaining me?' he demanded.

'Then why are you here?' She held her breath.

'If you want the truth…'

'And I do,' she assured him.

'You're the only person I can relax with, Mia.'

Was that a good thing? Or did it mean Ram took her for granted? She decided to call his bluff. 'Relax away—just don't mind me if I start snoring.'

His response was a low, sexy laugh. 'I don't think there's much chance of that, do you?'

Truthfully? None. But there was no need to let Ram think he could have everything his own way. But then it was Ram who changed the tone.

'There are dozens—maybe hundreds of petitioners already waiting in line outside. Some with justifiable concerns and others who are just trying to curry favour.'

'I'm sure you can tell them apart.'

'I'm sure I can too, but it doesn't make the numbers go away.'

'You'll have to make a list—prioritise.'

'Will I?' he said. His lips pressed down with amusement as he turned to stare at her.

'Sorry.' Drawing up her knees, she wrapped her arms around them. 'I realise you know that—I just thought—'

'Okay, Miss Organisation,' he teased her gently. 'How are you getting on with your side of things?'

'Good.' She couldn't keep the enthusiasm out of her voice.

'And it's good to see you growing in confidence again.'

Thanks to you, she thought.

'It's all your own doing, Mia. Only you can have the power to believe in yourself. No one else can help you with that— What's this?' he said, noticing the discarded newspaper on the night stand.

She was mortified. And then relieved when she saw the expression on his face.

'I see you've been studying the front page,' he said. 'So what do you make of it?'

'I don't know what to make of it, to be honest,' Mia admitted, unsure whether she wanted to hear the truth about Ram standing between a solemn-looking girl and Leila's father.

'That shot was taken on the anniversary of Leila's death, some time ago.'

And now she felt as bad as she could. 'I'm so sorry—I didn't know—'

'How could you know?'

He sat up as she shuffled off the bed, still with the sheet around her.

'I owed it to Leila's family to pay my respects,' he said to her back. 'And before you run away with the idea that Leila's younger sister has stepped into her place, let me reassure you that would never happen. I don't want her. I want you.'

She froze.

'I don't want all the old traditions either—I want to keep the best of the old and marry them with the new. Mia?' Ram prompted, tracing a shimmering line down the inside of her arm. 'Won't you come back to bed?'

It didn't seem the right time, and she still needed to find her level with Ram. Plaything wasn't enough—not the way she felt about him. 'Okay, but no sex,' she said stiffly.

'But I've explained everything to you.'

'Yes, you have, but you still treat me like a toy to be played with whenever you happen to have a spare moment.'

'And here was me thinking you liked me to play with you.' Catching hold of her wrist, he pressed his lips to the tender underside of it, making it hard for her to think, let alone speak.

'Are you totally without scruples?' she demanded tensely.

'Yes.'

Ram could always be relied on to be blunt. And she could always be relied on to respond to him. She could smell his warm, spicy man scent and her body was already on fire for his touch. She could smell the soap from his shower and knew his hair would still be damp—

But her decision had been made.

She climbed back into bed.

Ram hummed as she settled her head onto the pillow. 'The fact that you're pulling the sheet *up* has not escaped my notice.'

'I have work to do tomorrow, Ram, and some of us need our beauty sleep.'

'But not you,' he murmured, toying with a lock of her hair.

'Ram...'

'Do you seriously want me to change?'

'Why don't we talk? Tell me about your day.'

'Like an old married couple?'

'No, like friends—like friends who care about each other and want to share the good times and the bad.'

'Talking of bad. Do you really want this relationship without sex?'

'That's not bad, it's just different.'

He laughed. 'Are you sure you've thought it through?'

'Not completely.'

'I'd never have guessed,' he said dryly. 'So, what would rock your boat, Mia? Let's just say someone was interested in pursuing you with a view to taking things further?'

'An old-fashioned courtship might be acceptable.'

Ram hummed. 'Like someone to read poetry to you?'

'Are you mocking me?' she said suspiciously.

'Not at all,' Ram exclaimed. 'As if I would.'

But she had only relaxed on the pillow for a moment when he started spouting verse.

'"*Ah Love! could thou and I with Fate conspire to grasp this sorry scheme of things entire, would we not shatter it to bits—and then remould it nearer to the heart's desire?"* Omar Khayyam,' he explained smugly. 'That should do it.'

She stared at him blankly.

'You should read more poetry,' Ram insisted.

'And you should go to bed. Your brain is clearly over-heating.'

'Like other parts of my body,' he complained, 'but as you won't help me out—'

'Help you out?' Mia shot up. 'That's my point exactly. I am not some sort of super-charged sex toy.'

'But you are,' Ram disagreed with an unrepentant grin.

'Get out of here!' Mia exclaimed, flinging her pillows at his head.

'Delighted to. Oh, and I've arranged some time for us to-morrow—or, should I say today—so we'll make a start then, shall we?'

'A start on what?'

'Our courtship…'

Was it her fault the wedding march started clanging in her head? Or was that a warning bell?

Was Ram serious?

Hmm. Time would tell. 'So what form will this courtship take?' she said suspiciously.

'We'll take a walk. Look at the scenery. Gaze at the sunset. Stare into each other's eyes—we can even share a little music.'

'If you think I'm going to stand calmly by while you bawl your way through every rugby anthem you ever learned at school—'

'Okay, no rugby songs,' he agreed. 'I can see this is going to take quite a lot of forward planning.'

And now she had to bury her face in the bedclothes just to hide her smile. 'No one said you had to turn all serious on me.'

'And no one said you had to turn all frigid on me.'

'But I'm—'

'Not frigid?' Ram placed his finger over her lips. 'That's for you to prove and me to find out.' And then he pulled away. 'Goodnight, Mia—'

'*What?*' She sat up in bed, all thoughts of chastity and modesty forgotten. 'Where do you think you're going?'

'To make some plans.' Pausing by the door, Ram smiled his sexy smile. 'I should have thought of this sooner. Tomorrow, Mia…'

'You—'

Can't leave me, she had been about to say.

But he so obviously could.

CHAPTER EIGHTEEN

RAM could do courtly better than anyone she knew. In fact, he had probably majored in Courtology at university, Mia reflected as they walked together down a tree-shaded avenue. They were in the majestic gardens of the old palace, currently being followed by around twenty female members of staff, who thankfully kept a discreet distance from their robe-clad leader and his business-suited companion. Ram had knocked on Mia's door that morning with an offer for 'some stress relief before her next stint in front of the committee'. She should have known what that entailed, Mia realised, wincing, as Ram bellowed, "'Awake!'"

'*What?*' She recoiled back.

'Don't say what—say pardon,' he said sternly. 'I'm quoting poetry and you're spoiling the moment.'

'Apologies,' she said, playing along—though how she was supposed to keep a straight face when a man who looked more like a warrior than a poet was having a theatrical moment, she had no idea.

On the serious side, each time she saw Ram it seemed he had claimed back a little more of his heritage, and there was no doubt that in Ramprakeshi clothes he looked magnificent. The flowing night-dark blue silk robe he was wearing today hinted at his muscular form without revealing it, while the wristbands studded with rubies and diamonds only served to emphasise his brazen masculinity. Plus, he was wearing a jewelled belt with the biggest sword she had ever seen in her life hanging from it. 'Are we expecting an execution today?'

'We may well be if you don't shut up.'

'Okay, I guess this is your moment in the spotlight,' Mia conceded as a beam of sunlight caught them both in the face.

She didn't have to wait long.

"'Awake! For morning in the bowl of night has flung the stone that puts the stars to flight: And lo! the Hunter of the East has caught the Sultan's turret in a noose of light.'"

'But you're a maharaja,' she observed flatly.

'For goodness' sake,' Ram said, snapping the book shut and handing it to one of the many hovering servants, 'some people are never satisfied—'

'And are never likely to be if you continue reading poetry,' Mia muttered.

'And I thought a platonic courtship was what you wanted,' Ram protested, adopting a hurt expression. 'Now let me see—what comes after poetry? Ah, yes, music.'

'If you start singing I really shall run back to the palace.'

'What if I call for my lute?'

'Remembering the way you loved to torture my lute I'm more likely to hit you over the head with it.'

'I could get someone to play it for me.'

'I don't think so, Ram.'

'You're such a hard woman to please.'

'Since when?'

'Since you vowed off sex and demanded a more traditional approach.'

'Ram, this approach isn't traditional.'

'Didn't I warn you I'd be setting my own traditions?'

'You promised me stress relief earlier today,' Mia pointed out as Ram nudged her off the main boulevard onto a narrow path made almost completely invisible to those not in the know thanks to an abundance of raspberry-scented blossom.

'You're quite right—and I have the best idea for that.'

When things were going the way she thought she wanted them to she didn't like it. So when things started going the way she definitely didn't want them to she should like it even less—right?

Wrong, Mia discovered as Ram took her wrist in a firm grip and hurried her away from his attendants, pushing branches heavy with blossom aside as he took her deeper into the forest of concealing trees.

Predictably, she was instantly on fire for him. 'No, Ram—no. I mean it,' she protested. 'I'm warning you—'

'Would you refuse the attentions of your Lord and Master?'

'You bet I would,' she assured him as Ram backed her into an exquisitely ornamented garden room and shut the door.

Leaning back against it, he demanded, 'Even if you knew those attentions were good for you?'

'This is good for me?' she said, pretending surprise as Ram quickly dispensed with her skirt and briefs.

'This is the promised stress relief activity,' he murmured, 'though you'll have to promise not to scream too loud. The ladies know to stay on the avenue, but they're not deaf.'

'And so what are we supposed to be doing in here?'

'What maharajas and their ladies have been doing here for millennia.'

Heat exploded inside her as Ram backed her up against the wall. 'I said no sex,' she protested, scrambling up him.

'That was last night—and this is purely for therapeutic reasons,' Ram explained, thrusting his sword aside.

'Ah—oh—yes—I think you may be right,' Mia said, drowning in sensation as Ram secured her buttocks in his big, strong hands and took her deep. 'So it doesn't count,' she confirmed shakily as he began to move.

'Not at all. Feel free to enjoy it.'

'And afterwards it will be as if it never happened?'

'There's only so much my ego can take. Now concentrate,

will you? We don't want you to be late for your appointment
with the design committee.'

Concentrate? She was already there. *I think I love you*, she
thought. Or did she scream that too?

Mia got together with Ram in his private office after her
design meeting with his committee.

'You haven't got all the proper funding in place yet, Mia,'
Ram pointed out. 'Or the experience to handle the interior
design of both the house and the yacht.'

'Okay, you win,' she shouted, dropping her files on the top
of his desk. 'I give up—'

'No, you don't,' Ram ground out, baiting her with a stare.
'You never expected this to be easy—but that doesn't mean
you give up.'

'All right, I don't. But if I'm forced to work with several
other design companies, then I'm going to insist I stay on here
in Ramprakesh to be sure my ideas are handled properly.'

'Oh, no.' Ram had difficulty curbing his smile. 'You can't
be serious about staying on? How will I survive it?' He caught
the tiny furled hand and brought it to his lips before Mia
could waste any more of her energy pounding on him. 'Don't
you know I want you here?' he murmured, brushing his lips
against her neck.

'What? As your royal concubine—I don't think so,
Ram.'

'I wasn't thinking of a post that allowed for quite so much
time off—I was thinking more…royal project manager?'

'Isn't that like a catch-all term for a gofer?'

'Well, I can think of plenty of things you can go for—and
come for, now I think about it.'

'Will you stop that?' Mia demanded, finding she couldn't
stop her smile either. Just the thought of being with Ram—
working again at a job she loved—was enough to make her
deliriously happy. 'I realise this is the right decision for me
to make from a professional point of view—I still have a lot

to learn—and you can stop looking at me as if you want to say I told you so.'

'Would I do that?'

'Anyone who can wind me up with that play-act of a court-ship is capable of anything.'

'But I was being serious,' he insisted.

'Yeah, right. And you can stop trying to destress me too—we both know where that leads.'

'Well, I'm glad you've decided to stay. I think we're on the brink of something really exciting in Ramprakesh.'

'The birth of a new Golden Age?'

'You can call it that.'

'It could be if we make it so,' Mia agreed thoughtfully. 'Do you really think we can?' She stared out across the terracotta rooftops over a magical kingdom of towering golden cupolas and slender ivory towers.

'I wouldn't be here if I didn't believe that,' Ram said, turning serious. 'And with your designs and my determination—'

'With *my* determination, and your money—'

'Gold-digger—'

'Scrooge—'

'Shameless hussy—'

'I'll settle for that—'

'No, you won't,' Ram insisted, and, taking hold of her hands, he stared deep into Mia's eyes. 'You're far too special to talk about yourself like that. And when I take a wife—'

Heaving a sigh, she cut across him. 'Criteria?' She didn't want to go there—but she couldn't escape the fact that one day Ram would take a wife.

'Criteria?' he said. 'What do you mean?'

'Well, you gave me the post of royal project manager, so who else is going to sort out a wife for you?'

'Good point,' Ram agreed. 'I'd better come up with a few pointers for you… Let's start with a good homemaker—then, someone as wise as she is beautiful…someone strong enough

to support and defend her family as well as my country…
someone I can rub along with, naturally—'

'But not in the garden room,' Mia warned. 'Naturally, or
not, that's our place, Ram.'

'For clandestine meetings.' His lips pressed down as he
thought about it. 'I like your thinking.'

'You're supposed to be taking this seriously.'

'Believe me, I am. Now, would you like me to show you
your new office?'

'An office for me here at the palace?' she exclaimed with
surprise.

It was nice to catch Mia on the wrong foot occasionally.
'Of course—until you've designed a new one for yourself at
my new home.'

She'd need one there in order to supervise the design work,
Mia reasoned. 'Okay,' she said, her curiosity thoroughly
piqued by now. 'You'd better lead the way…'

It was all packing cases and chaos inside her new office at the
palace and Mia was amazed to discover that her brother had
already sent over everything she had ever cared for that was
connected to her passion for design—all the books, all the
trade articles, the posters and magazines, all the newspaper
clippings. 'How did Tom know to do this?'

'We spoke on the phone,' Ram said, dipping his head to
stare at her. 'You can't expect us to cease all communications
just because I've been seeing you, Mia. Your brother and I
have been close since we were boys and nothing's going to
change that. Plus we both love you—'

'In your own very distinct ways,' she agreed, making light
of Ram's careless choice of words. 'Well, it's fantastic and I'm
thrilled—but who paid for all the rest of it?' She was picking
her way between some very impressive equipment as well as
new furniture.

'A friend of yours—'

'You?'

'Don't look so scandalised. I expect you to pay me back when you become successful—which you will be.'

'You've got a lot of confidence in me—I only hope it isn't misplaced.'

'That's up to you, Mia. I'm not doing you any favours. You've earned the chance to do this and now you have to earn the right to stay.'

She turned an amused glance his way. 'There's nothing like lacing a challenge with a hefty dose of threat.'

'Would you have it any other way? You never wanted things easy. Hey, stop that,' he said as she absent-mindedly traced her scars. 'I don't want to see you do that ever again. Do you understand me?'

His voice was so fierce she snatched her hand away.

And then Ram completely distracted her when he began to rifle through the tower of packages on her new and extremely impressive desk. 'Why don't you let the royal project manager find whatever it is you're looking for?'

'This is a job for an expert,' he insisted, tossing stuff aside. 'I feel a musical moment coming on.'

And a light went on in her brain. 'If that wretched lute has found its way in here,' she threatened, joining him in the sea of bubble wrap and cardboard, 'it can go straight back home.'

She narrowed her eyes suspiciously as Ram pulled back. 'Go, find, tiger,' he murmured.

'I knew it,' Mia exclaimed, spotting a tell-tale slender wooden neck. 'You know what I said—and I jolly well mean it. If you start twanging that thing in here I'll beat you over the head with it. Give it to me,' she warned as Ram held the instrument over her head.

But when she snatched it from him something jangled inside it. 'Oh, no... Don't tell me I've broken it.' She might not want Ram to play the old lute, but it was a family heirloom, and she'd had it as a sort of lucky charm in her room growing up. And now she could see that highly decorated filigree rose carved by a craftsman into the wood was missing from the centre of the soundboard. 'Did I do that?'

'I don't know—did you?'

'I'm not sure.' Mia examined the gaping hole again and groaned. 'Surely I couldn't have been so careless.'

Ram remained silent.

'It's such a big hole.' She threw an anguished glance his way.

'And?'

'And it sounds as if it might have a screw loose.'

'No, that would be me,' Ram argued as Mia plunged her tiny fingers inside the hole to remove the foreign body.

'What's this?' she said, staring with amazement at the enormous blue-white diamond she had just pulled out on its jewelled band.

'It looks like a ring to me—just an observation,' Ram said, holding up his hands in mock-surrender.

'It is a ring,' she said stupidly. 'But what's it doing here? Do you think it's been here long? Ram…? Ram!' Mia's jaw dropped. Shock had made her somewhat slower than usual.

Removing the ring from her, Ram reached for her hand.

'Are you—? Is this…?' she blurted.

'A proposal?' he said coolly as he selected Mia's marriage finger. 'Yes, it is.'

'Well, down on one knee, then.'

There was a moment and then they both laughed. And Ram, for maybe the first time in his life, did as he was told.

'Mia Spencer-Dayly, I have loved you since the first day I set eyes on you, and over the years that love has deepened. And now I realise that I can't live without you—which is a damn nuisance, actually, because now I shall have to marry you.'

She huffed. 'Don't let me force you.'

But Ram was serious. 'Will you marry me, Mia?'

'You're sure about this?'

'I am,' he said.

Mia stared at Ram, hardly able to comprehend the enormity of the moment. Having dreamed of this all her life, now the moment had come she was lost for words. 'Is that it?' she managed finally.

Ram looked thoughtful for a moment. 'Were you expecting something more?'

'Oh, I don't know...' *Jewelled steeples twinkling in the fast-fading light against an indigo sky... Drums—bells— horn-blowing, perhaps? Incense wafting. Rose-petal flinging, potentially? Elephants? Definitely—* But it was time to stop day-dreaming. 'No, of course I wasn't expecting anything more—and I'm deeply honoured...'

'Honoured? I don't want to be honoured. I want you to love me—'

'Love you? I adore you.'

'Not as much as I adore you.'

'Do we have to fight over that as well?'

Ram's answer was to brush his lips against her neck. And then she thought of something else. 'I was just thinking—'

'Oh, no,' he groaned, 'not that again.'

'Seriously, Ram, what about tradition? Would your people welcome me?'

'You're right—we'd better check,' he said, looking serious. Holding out his hand, he drew her outside onto the balcony.

'Is this for me?' Mia exclaimed as the first fireworks lit up the sky.

'This is for us,' Ram said as tiny lights showered down from the sky like so many sparkling wishes. 'You're the love of my life, Mia, and my people share my happiness. All I want is to keep you safe.'

'But not too safe, I hope?' she said, turning to look at him.

'What's wrong with being safe?'

'*Too safe* would rule you out,' she said, and then she clung to him as if she would never let him go as the first faint sounds of bells and drums and horns heralded the arrival of the elephant parade.

CHAPTER NINETEEN

THE night before her wedding was wonderfully smoky and mysterious. She was leaning over the balcony, watching visitors arrive, grateful that the moon had come out to brush the shadows from the sky. There was to be a grand ball at the old palace on the hill before Mia was taken to the house of the women to be prepared for her lover, who would shortly become both her husband as well as the acknowledged leader of a country on the brink of great and wonderful change.

And Ram had arranged one more surprise, Mia realised with a shriek of excitement as the door to her apartment crashed open and the five crazy women who were to act as her bridesmaids piled in a good few hours ahead of schedule.

'Surprise!' they chorused, spreading out across the vast acreage of marble floor, shooting coats, bags, scarves and magazines in every direction.

'It's not like you lot to be early,' Mia exclaimed as they shared a group hug.

'And it's not like you to marry a maharaja,' Xheni observed, exchanging glances with the other girls.

'Now you know Ram's given up the title,' Mia protested.

'But his people wouldn't let him go—so nothing's changed,' Xheni said with a shrug. 'You can change the title, but you can't change the man—'

And thank goodness for it, Mia thought.

'Perhaps we should try and calm things down a bit,' Xheni

suggested, tongue in cheek as she practised a queenly wave in front of one of the mirrors. 'This is a royal establishment, is it not?' she demanded, turning to sweep Mia a low curtsey.

'Will you stop that?' Mia demanded, laughing with the rest of the girls when, following Xheni's lead, they began bowing to each other and strutting around the room with their noses in the air. 'None of this changes me.'

'Well, it damn well should do,' Xheni protested. 'I expect you to bestow all sorts of titles on me as soon as you are enthroned.'

'First off, I'm getting married, not enthroned—and secondly, there are no titles in Ramprakesh these days.'

'Well, that's a shame, isn't it, girls? I wouldn't have come if I'd known,' Xheni exclaimed.

'Neither would we,' they chorused on cue.

'So, where's the Ram?' Xheni demanded, swinging her long legs as she perched on a side table, stuffing as many handmade chocolates into her mouth as would fit.

'Ram is resting quietly.'

'Yeah, I bet he is,' Xheni scoffed to a chorus of raucous laughter.

'No, seriously,' Mia insisted, trying for prim. 'The most recent of Ram's *new* traditions insists the bride and groom must remain celibate on the night before the wedding.'

'I think he's having you on,' Xheni commented, helping herself to another handful of chocolate.

'Not at all,' Mia insisted. 'Ram would never do that.'

She had to pause while Xheni scoffed at that and almost choked.

'We'll meet briefly at the ball—well chaperoned, of course—and then we'll go our separate ways.'

'I can't believe you fell for it.'

'I didn't fall for anything.'

'Right,' Xheni drawled, exchanging glances with the other girls. 'You see what happens when you fall in love, girls? You lose your edge.'

'This time you're wrong,' Mia said confidently. 'And, anyway, what are we arguing about? Let's have some pre-wedding fun.'

'We're up for that,' the girls exclaimed.

'And we have a secret weapon,' Xheni confided. 'Girls,' she said with some ceremony, 'The Dress...'

'But I already have a ball gown,' Mia pointed out, thoroughly confused now.

'Oh, that old thing,' Xheni exclaimed, dismissing the designer gown Mia had bought especially for the night-before-the-wedding party with a flick of her wrist. 'We have something much better, don't we, girls?'

Mia drew in a sharp breath when she recognised the gown box they were carrying. 'You remembered...'

'That's what friends are for,' Xheni said. 'Lucky for you your mother kept the gown Ram bought you all these years ago.'

And so Mia had the opportunity to untie the black silk bow on the powder-pink gown box a second time. Lifting out the exquisite dress to sighs of appreciation from the girls, she held it in front of her. 'I hope it still fits.'

'Of course it will fit,' they insisted, while Xheni added that certain film stars she knew would die for a chance to wear the famous French designer's iconic column of beaded, flesh-coloured silk.

To Mia's relief, the dress fitted like a second skin, and was possibly the most beautiful gown on earth.

'You mean it's taken you all this time to realise Ram has always been in love with you?' Xheni demanded, looking at how the dress transformed her friend.

The girls shared Xheni's huff of disbelief, and even Mia was forced to wind back the reel and remember the looks Ram used to give her, looks she had taken for teasing or provoking her—anything but desire, let alone love. And this time when she stood in front of the mirror imagining Ram holding her

it was quite something to know she had the best chance ever
of making that dream come true.

And as for Ram's new traditions? She had a few of her own
in mind, Mia concluded, smiling a secret smile.

She stole his breath away. All his good intentions went up in
smoke the instant Mia entered the ballroom. 'You look amazing,' he said, claiming her instantly.

Leading Mia down the wide sweep of marble stairs into
the heart of the crowded ballroom, he could feel his hackles
rising as every man present fixed his gaze on Mia. 'I can't
believe you're wearing the dress I bought you...'

'At least you can't accuse me of being extravagant.'

'But I can accuse you of being so beautiful I have to take
you straight to bed.'

'Then why don't you?' Mia murmured as Ram greeted
her girlfriends, who were waiting in line with all the other
dignitaries at the foot of the stairs.

'Because I have to dance with you first,' he growled
discreetly.

'Oh, no... Surely we shouldn't risk touching each other on
the night before our wedding?'

'We may have to—if only to stop you being trampled in
the stampede.'

'Do you think other men might want to dance with me?'

'I know they do,' Ram murmured, sweeping Mia into his
arms.

He guided her effortlessly through the other couples who
were now joining them on the dance floor, heading straight
towards an open door.

'Where are you taking me?' Mia queried.

'I had intended to suggest you relax on the sidelines tonight—conserve your energy for our honeymoon. But now I
feel the overriding need for certain activities that cannot be
accomplished without your active participation.'

'Oh, dear,' she said, pretending alarm. 'Do I take it you have an escape plan?'

'I do...'

The howdah that was to take Mia to the wedding ceremony the following morning was already down in the courtyard where it seemed so much bigger than it had done when it was positioned on the back of a mighty elephant. Draped in crimson velvet and surrounded by golden screens, it promised delicious privacy.

'I think we should test it, just to be sure it suits your every need,' Ram murmured, drawing one curtain aside.

Mia didn't need asking twice.

Sinking into feather cushions covered in the softest of fabrics was a sensual high only Ram could have devised, she decided contentedly. Having Ram join her—feeling him hard and strong, and indecently virile as he pressed against her, was—

'Is this the place?'

Mia jumped with alarm as a voice she would have known anywhere invaded her love nest.

'Ah, yes, I see it is.'

And now a cane she would have known anywhere insinuated itself between the velvet folds and neatly flipped back the curtains concealing her from the world. 'Monsieur Michel!' she shrieked, glancing in shock from her old employer to Ram.

Mia's eyes narrowed. 'You planned this,' she accused Ram in a discreet whisper as he swung out of the howdah to greet their newly arrived guest. 'It's just another of my new traditions,' Ram informed her, ducking his head back in briefly to share this information. 'Abstinence is good for you, Mia. You'll learn to thank me in time.'

She doubted it. A full twenty-four hours until she felt Ram's hands on her body again?

But now she had to remember her manners. 'Monsieur

Michel,' she said, climbing out of the howdah. Once she had got over the shock Mia was genuinely thrilled to see her elderly employer, and recovered her composure in time to exchange the customary kisses on each cheek. 'How wonderful to see you, Monsieur. Welcome to Ramprakesh.'

'The home of passion *and* restraint,' Ram added dryly, shooting a veiled look at Mia.

A temple shimmering in the moonlight was to host both Mia's preparations to become Ram's bride and her wedding night. She had been carried there in the howdah on the back of an elephant in the middle of a torchlit procession, which Ram explained signified light cutting through the darkness and removing all bad thoughts from the world. This was just one of many rituals that had been passed down intact through the generations over thousands of years, and it made Mia feel as if an unbroken link from the past were reaching out to welcome her.

'There is no better guidance for life than the wisdom of Ramprakesh,' the ladies detailed to wait on Mia told her as they bustled about. Having bathed her and sugared her skin to remove every trace of hair they had massaged her with scented oils until her skin took on a luminous glow, and now they were decorating her hands and feet with intricate swirls of henna.

Having thanked them, Mia invited them to eat and drink the delicacies that had been prepared for her. She couldn't eat a single thing—she was too busy counting the hours, minutes and the seconds until she could be alone with Ram. No one understood the benefit of delay better than he did, but a week-long ceremony leading up to their actual marriage and then finally the wedding night, when she was only supposed to catch a glimpse of him in passing, was overdoing things a bit, in Mia's opinion, and should have been the first of the traditions that Ram changed.

She almost cried with relief when the ladies declared it

was time to dress her in the ruby-red chiffon sari and veil she had chosen for the wedding ceremony. Minutes later, or so it seemed, she was standing beneath a tented canopy with Ram resplendent at her side in heavily decorated black silk, accepting and making vows to stand at his side for ever.

'Husband and wife at last,' he murmured as he led her at a stately pace through their guests.

'Can't you send everyone away so we can be alone?' she murmured, wondering if it was possible to die from frustration.

'Are you naked beneath your sari?'

'Is your name Knucklehead?'

'According to you, it is.'

Mia fixed her gaze on the golden doors that led to the wedding and bedding suite, as Ram had jokingly referred to their accommodation for this very special jewel-coloured night. 'I'm completely naked,' she assured him.

They barely made it through the doors before Ram's mouth swooped down on hers, igniting flash-points on every part of her body. Slamming the door closed, he dropped the bolt. Meanwhile, Mia was learning that certain Ramprakeshi traditions weren't so bad—especially the way a man's traditional robe fell to the ground when you undid a fastening or two.

'Do you realise you're growling as you undress me?' Ram chided her with a laugh.

'Are you surprised when you've kept me away from all this?' Kicking his robe aside, she basked in the jaw-dropping good looks of the man standing brazenly naked in front of her.

'Your turn next,' he insisted as he deftly freed the ties holding Mia's sari in place.

Turning like a dancer as he unwound it, she felt like a dervish desperate to be free. 'At last!' she exclaimed as he tossed the yards of fabric aside.

'Indeed,' Ram agreed, admiring her. 'But what did I tell you about the benefits of delay?'

'Don't tell me about it,' Mia insisted. 'Prove it.'

'That will be my pleasure.'

'And mine,' Mia assured him, taking Ram boldly in her hand.

They didn't make it to the bed.

'And now it's time to exchange wedding presents,' Ram insisted when they had taken a shower and were both wrapped in towels and sitting side by side on the bed.

'What on earth's this?' Mia demanded when he handed her a long, bulky package that must have taken a whole reel of sticky tape to hold together.

'Why don't you open it and find out?'

'I hope you haven't been too extravagant,' Mia warned as Ram slanted her one of his sexy, teasing looks.

'I haven't been extravagant at all,' he assured her. 'Stop yapping and open it.'

'Okay...' She ripped at the paper and thigh-high boots fell out. 'What...?'

'Did I ever say I didn't like your pirate costume?' Ram's grin was wicked. 'I'm looking forward to some rather exciting private exhibitions by the infamous Arabella Drummond.'

With a cry of pretended disapproval Mia fell on him, kissing and punching him, and loving him with all her heart. 'You have a one-track mind, Ram Varindha.'

'Yes...full of you,' he said. 'We're going to have such fun, Mia. I know I'm asking a lot of you—new home, new career, new public responsibilities—but I want you to know that we'll always make time for you and me...'

'Fun, you said?' Mia said when Ram finally released her.

'You have no idea,' he promised.

'I have some,' she argued. 'But not too much fun for you, rich boy.'

'Meaning?' Ram said suspiciously, shooting a glance at

Mia's long legs flailing about as she reached underneath the bed.

'I have something for you,' she said, emerging triumphant.

'What's this?' Ram said, laughing as she handed him a full racing kit complete with helmet.

'So, what do you think of your new logo?'

Ram could only shake with laughter. Gone was the naked woman, and in her place was a pirate queen complete with eyepatch and a very dangerous expression indeed on her face.

MILLS & BOON®
HAVE JOINED FORCES
WITH THE LEANDER TRUST
AND LEANDER CLUB TO HELP
TO DEVELOP TOMORROW'S
CHAMPIONS

We have produced a stunning calendar for 2011 featuring a host of Olympic and World Champions (as they've never been seen before!). Leander Club is recognised the world over for its extraordinary rowing achievements and is committed to developing its squad of athletes to help underpin future British success at World and Olympic level.

'All my rowing development has come through the support and back-up from Leander. The Club has taken me from a club rower to an Olympic Silver Medallist. Leander has been the driving force behind my progress'

RIC EGINGTON – Captain, Leander Club Olympic Silver, Beijing, 2009 World Champion.

Please send me ☐ calendar(s) @ £8.99 each plus £3.00 P&P (FREE postage and packing on orders of 3 or more calendars despatching to the same address).

I enclose a cheque for £ _____ made payable to Harlequin Mills & Boon Limited.

Name _____

Address _____

_____ Post code _____

Email _____

Send this whole page and cheque to:
Leander Calendar Offer
Harlequin Mills & Boon Limited
Eton House, 18-24 Paradise Road, Richmond TW9 1SR

All proceeds from the sale of the 2011 Leander Fundraising Calendar will go towards the Leander Trust (Registered Charity No: 284631) – and help in supporting aspiring athletes to train to their full potential.

MILLS & BOON®

are proud to present our...

Book of the Month

★ The Accidental Princess
by Michelle Willingham
from Mills & Boon® Historical

Etiquette demands Lady Hannah Chesterfield ignore
the shivers of desire Lieutenant Michael Thorpe's
wicked gaze provokes, but her unawakened body
clamours for his touch… So she joins Michael on
an adventure to uncover the secret of his birth—
is this common soldier really a prince?

Available 5th November

*Something to say about our
Book of the Month?
Tell us what you think!*

millsandboon.co.uk/community
facebook.com/romancehq
twitter.com/millsandboonuk

All the magic you'll need this Christmas...

Angels in the Snow

Do fairy lights and family
make the perfect Christmas?

Sarah Morgan

When **Daniel** is left with his brother's kids, only
one person can help. But it'll take more than
mistletoe before **Stella** helps him...

Patrick hadn't advertised for a housekeeper. But
when **Hayley** appears, she's the gift he didn't
even realise he needed.

Alfie and his little sister know a lot about the magic
of Christmas – and they're about to teach the
grown-ups a much-needed lesson!

Available 1st October 2010

1210/10/MB315

A season for
falling in love...

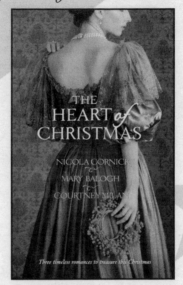

THE
HEART *of*
CHRISTMAS

NICOLA CORNICK
~
MARY BALOGH
~
COURTNEY MILAN

Three timeless romances to treasure this Christmas

Bestselling author Mary Balogh presents
A Handful of Gold

Join Nicola Cornick for
The Season for Suitors

Courtney Milan offers
This Wicked Gift

Available 19th November 2010

www.millsandboon.co.uk

Meet Nora Robert's
The MacGregors family

1st October 2010

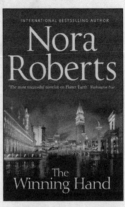

3rd December 2010

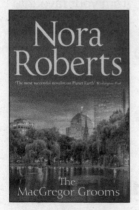

7th January 2011

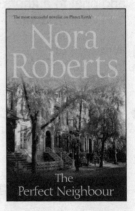

4th February 2011